Kid Palomino: Outlaws

Outlaw Bill Carson and his gang ride into the quiet settlement of Fargo knowing that the sheriff and his deputies are out of town. Carson has inside information about the bank and banker, which the ruthless killer intends to use to his advantage. What Carson and his equally blood-thirsty gang do not know is that the deputies have arrived back early. Kid Palomino and his fellow lawman Red Rivers notice the strangers in town and decide to find out who they are. All hell erupts as the lawmen confront Carson and his gang. The Kid and Red give chase. . . .

By the same author

The Valko Kid
Kid Palomino
The Guns of Trask
The Shadow of Valko
Palomino Rider
The Spurs of Palomino
South of the Badlands
The Masked Man
Palomino Showdown
Return of the Valko Kid
The Trail of Trask
Kid Dynamite
War Smoke
The Sunset Kid
The Venom of Valko
The Mark of Trask
Fortress Palomino
To Kill the Valko Kid
Kid Fury
Stagecoach to Waco Wells
The Ghosts of War Smoke
The Wizard of War Smoke

Kid Palomino: Outlaws

Michael D. George

ROBERT HALE

First published in Great Britain 2017

ISBN 978-0-7198-2198-1

The Crowood Press
The Stable Block
Crowood Lane
Ramsbury
Marlborough
Wiltshire SN8 2HR

www.bhwesterns.com

Robert Hale is an imprint
of The Crowood Press

Typeset by
Derek Doyle & Associates, Shaw Heath
Printed and bound in Great Britain by
CPI Group (UK) Ltd, Croydon, CR0 4YY

Dedicated to my grand-daughters Alexia and Skye

PROLOGUE

The town of Fargo was quiet. Most of its inhabitants had been asleep for hours as the sky slowly began to show the first glimpses of light. The sun was about to rise but five riders were already wide-awake as they slowly steered their horses into the sleepy settlement. Merciless outlaw Bill Carson led his band of fellow outlaws through the back streets toward the Fargo Bank.

Like his followers, Carson sported a long dust coat which hid their arsenal of weaponry from curious eyes. He led the Brand brothers, Luke and Amos through the shadows like a mute army general. Poke Peters and Jeff Kane trailed the trio like obedient guard dogs. It was their job to watch out for any sign of trouble that might raise its head and start fanning their gun hammers in their direction.

Yet Fargo was a law-abiding settlement. Trouble rarely entered its boundaries. Until this day it had only had to cope with drunken revelry but as the heavens slowly grew lighter above the roof shingles, all that was about to change. Had it been later in the day, the streets would have been filled to overflowing with people going about their rituals.

Bill Carson had chosen the moment of their arrival with perfect accuracy. He knew that the moment between night and the birth of a new day was when all towns were at their most vulnerable.

The outlaw leader kept tapping his bloody spurs into the flanks of his powerful mount. Carson was known for his prowess at robbing even the sturdiest of banks and was wanted dead or alive in three states and two territories. Yet no one in Fargo had ever set eyes upon him before. He had travelled more than a hundred miles from his usual hunting grounds in order to strike at Fargo's seemingly impenetrable bank.

Unknown to his four deadly underlings, Carson had been given inside information concerning not only the bank itself but also its owner. All the brutal Carson had to do was follow his instructions and the money was as good as his.

The five riders continued at their slow pace and as far as Carson was concerned, everything else would fall neatly into place. His hooded eyes glanced over his shoulder at the men riding behind him. They were all hired killers and wanted by the law just like he was. The only difference between them was that Carson demanded total obedience and would kill even them if they did not follow his orders.

Carson had two rules that he demanded his followers abide by without question.

The first was to kill anyone who got in their way and the second was not to show any mercy. Carson had earned the high price on his head. He had left a mountain of dead bodies in his wake. Women and children fared little better than men when it came to the hot lead he and his men dished out.

Carson glanced at the cloudless heavens and continued to jab his spurs into his walking mount. Blood dripped from the metal spikes. He watched the sky turn pink as the distant sun was about to rise.

The bank stood like a fortress in the middle of Fargo. It towered over the many other buildings. Not one of the numerous outlaws who had passed this way before had even dared to try and rob it. Its red brick and cement walls were enough to scare most of the lethal outlaws away. The iron bars that covered every one of its windows looked impossible to penetrate, as did its reinforced doors.

Yet Bill Carson kept jabbing his spurs even though

he knew the bank was virtually impregnable. His eyes darted from one shadow to the next as he led his four followers deeper into the sprawling town. The empty streets satisfied the merciless Carson as he glanced at the gigantic edifice.

'Keep riding, boys,' he growled.

The five horsemen rode slowly past the massive structure and glanced at the ominous sight. Fargo was getting brighter with every heartbeat but Carson did not seem to be at all concerned. The confused riders who trailed the veteran bank robber considered the reason why the ruthless Carson continued to jab his spurs and turn into another side street.

The Brand brothers glanced at one another and silently began to wonder why they were now riding away from the very thing they had travelled two days to rob. Amos Brand looked over his shoulder at Peters and Kane. They too could not understand what was going on.

But no matter how curious they were they did not dare to question Carson's motives or reasoning. They just followed and left the thinking to the lethal outlaw.

Bill Carson turned up what appeared at first glance to be a dead end, yet the narrow lane led to a secluded street of four very expensive houses. Carson drew rein and stopped his mount as his gang flanked him.

'What's this place, Bill?' Luke Brand asked as he surveyed the properties curiously. 'Why'd we come here?'

'I thought we were here to rob that back there,' Kane added as he steadied his mount.

Carson did not answer. He simply pulled out a long thin cigar and bit off its tail. He spat at the ground and then placed the black weed between his teeth. Then the outlaw struck a match and cupped its flame and sucked. When his lungs were filled with acrid smoke, Carson slowly exhaled and tossed the match at the sand before them.

He pointed at the end house. 'See that house sitting there, boys?'

The four riders nodded.

'What's so important about that one, Bill?' Kane asked.

'A certain Stanley Hardwick lives in that fine house,' Carson informed his curious men. 'And Hardwick happens to be the man who owns that big red brick bank.'

Peters rested his hands on his saddle horn and looked blankly at Carson. 'That's real nice, Bill. But why do we wanna know where that varmint lives?'

Carson tilted his head, pulled the cigar from his mouth and tapped ash at the sand. A cruel smile etched his hardened features as he glared at Peters and then the others.

'Hardwick don't live on his lonesome,' he said. 'He got himself a wife and a fifteen-year-old daughter.'

His men were still no wiser. They looked at their leader with bemused expressions. Carson shook his head and sighed heavily.

'I happen to know this because a certain party told me all about the banker, boys,' he explained. 'Hardwick will do anything to save them females from being harmed. Now do you savvy?'

'Who told you, Bill?' Luke Brand asked.

'The man who plans all my jobs for me, Luke boy,' Carson sucked more smoke into his lungs. 'A critter that I've never even met but he's the smartest bastard this side of the Pecos.'

'What's his name?' Kane wondered.

Carson grunted with amusement. 'I'll tell you his name when the job is all done.'

Peters steadied his mount. 'I heard that they got themselves a pretty good bunch of star-packers in Fargo, Bill. What we gonna do when we have to face them critters?'

The outlaw leader muffled his amusement.

'I've bin told that they're out of town, Poke.' Carson grinned and concentrated on the house again. He looked at the affluent structure. 'They've got a retired old lawman holding the fort. He ain't gonna trouble us.'

A sense of relief drifted through the men behind Carson's wide shoulders. Amos Brand edged his horse closer to the older man and looked at Carson.

'You mean that Kid Palomino ain't in Fargo?' he asked nervously. 'That critter is said to have killed more lawbreakers than most. Are you sure he's out of town with the sheriff, Bill?'

Smoke drifted from Carson's mouth. 'I'm dead sure, Amos.'

'Phew,' the outlaw exhaled. 'I sure didn't hanker taking on Kid Palomino.'

Carson gathered his reins in his gloved hands.

'C'mon. We'll tie our horses around the back of that mighty fine house and then pay Hardwick a visit,' he said.

The sound of spurs filled the quiet street as the five horsemen encouraged their mounts on toward the banker's home.

ONE

Apart from the sound of distant roosters hailing the arrival of a new day, the five horsemen were totally alone in the quiet section of Fargo. The caravan snaked along the neatly maintained street and turned up behind the most imposing of all its houses. Carson was first to drop to the ground from his trail-weary horse and lash its long leathers to a white upright close to the rear of the banker's home. As his gloved hands tightened the reins his underlings dismounted around their merciless leader.

Bill Carson had learned long ago that it did not pay to have a regular gang of fellow outlaws. For even the best outlaws could and would betray their more famed leader given the chance. Each job required different skills and Carson always prided himself in choosing the right men for the right job.

So it was as the first rays of the day raced across the cloudless sky above Dry Gulch. The seasoned killer of untold numbers of men, women and children checked his pair of matched Remington .45s and glanced at his men.

His eyes were like emotionless ice. Their glare could cause most grown men to freeze when they focused upon them. The four hired guns he had recruited only a week earlier were no different. They each knew that Carson would kill any or all of them should he want.

'Take off your spurs,' Carson snarled quietly.

The four dust-caked men behind his wide shoulders did exactly as they were commanded and placed their spurs in their saddle-bags just as Carson had also done. He gave a nod of his head and turned on his heels.

The fearsome Carson led his men to the rear door of Hardwick's home and grabbed the door handle with his left hand as his right clutched his six-shooter at hip level.

The door was unlocked.

A wry grin etched his face as Carson looked back at his four followers.

'Folks are mighty trusting in Fargo, boys,' he hissed. 'Reckon it's time we taught them how dumb that is.'

The five hardened criminals entered quickly and spread out through the quiet house. None of the quintet had ever seen such obvious wealth before as they moved around the interior of Hardwick's home. It was everywhere they looked. Expensive paintings adorned the walls and lush imported carpets covered the highly polished floorboards.

Peters and Kane signalled to Carson that there was nobody on the ground floor as the Brand brothers glanced up the staircase like rabid wolves. The thought of the two females upstairs made both the depraved outlaws eager to get their hands upon them.

'Wipe the drool from your mouths,' Carson ordered the brothers. 'You can have your fun when the time's right and not a damn second before. Savvy?'

Both Brand brothers reluctantly nodded. Their desires were not as great as their fear of the veteran outlaw. Even though they had never worked with Carson before, they both knew of his reputation and it frightened them.

They nodded in silent obedience.

Carson moved between Amos and Luke and pointed up the carpeted staircase to the landing.

'Get them,' he ordered. 'Bring them down here and don't go using them hog-legs. I don't want any shooting to wake up this town.'

'We don't need our guns to round up a banker and his brood, Bill,' Amos said as he placed a boot on the first run of the steps.

'Get them,' Carson repeated.

As Peters and Kane moved back to the side of Carson, the Brand siblings slowly ascended the carpeted staircase. The thick pile of the carpet absorbed any sound of their hefty footwear. A few moments after the two men entered the bedrooms the noise of startled outrage filled the large house.

'I still can't figure out why we come here and not the bank, Bill,' Peters said as he stared up at the landing. 'Not unless this Hardwick critter has got himself a safe in this house.'

Carson raised his eyebrows. 'You'll understand soon enough, Poke.'

The noise of the younger female was the loudest but was soon muffled by the palm of one of the Brand brother's gloved hands.

Carson holstered his gun and listened with amusement to the activity up upon the landing as Amos and Luke rounded up the three members of the Hardwick family and began forcing them out of their bedrooms and toward the staircase.

As the sound of startled adults and the child grew louder above him, Carson's attention was suddenly drawn to the kitchen. His eyes narrowed.

'What was that, Bill?' Kane whispered.

Carson said nothing as his eyes narrowed and focused on the rear door in the kitchen. He turned and moved quickly into the large cooking area as the rear door was pushed open and a well-rounded woman entered. Her arms were full of parcels of differing shapes and sizes as she waddled toward a table.

It had not occurred to Carson that anyone as wealthy as Hardwick would have people working for him. His information had not gone into that sort of detail. The lethal outlaw pressed his back against the wall behind the rear door as the female shuffled across the tiled floor.

Elvira Baker was a woman in her mid-fifties. She had worked for the banker as his cook and cleaner for nearly a decade. She knew her duties and nothing had ever interfered with them.

Until now.

Now her entire world was about to come crashing down.

Elvira stopped and placed the groceries on to the rectangular table unaware of the intruders within the lavish house. As she placed the provisions on the table her attention was drawn to the muddy footprints on the tiles. Elvira stopped and stared at the floor in bewilderment.

'I only scrubbed them tiles last night,' she pondered as her mind raced. 'Who on earth dragged in that mud?'

The sound of the door being shut behind her filled her with a mix of fear and curiosity. Her eyes widened as she slowly turned around.

The sight of the tall outlaw standing across the door sent a chill through her.

'It's a bad habit talking to yourself,' Carson sneered. 'I'm told they lock folks up in asylums for less.'

Elvira's eyes widened as she stared in horror at the figure clad in the long dust coat. He towered above her petite form. She was about to speak when she noticed the gun belt and the gleaming .45s hidden beneath the protective coat.

The cook tried to swallow but it was impossible. Fear gripped her throat like a noose. She rested her hip against the table and tried to steady herself as fear washed over her startled shape.

'Who are you?' she managed to ask as her entire body shook with growing alarm.

The hideous smile grew wider across Carson's face. He began to approach her slowly. 'It ain't none of your business, woman.'

Elvira's eyes flashed. She turned and started to

make her way across the kitchen. After only three steps she saw the ominous figure of Poke Peters blocking her way into the living area of the house. She abruptly stopped as Carson continued to track her every step behind her.

She turned and looked up into Carson's narrowed eyes.

'Who are you?' she asked fearfully.

'I'm just someone who's got business with your boss,' Carson replied in a low drawl as he strode across the tiled floor and placed a hand on her shoulder. She looked up into his cold, calculating eyes as he smiled. For a moment the tone of his emotionless voice calmed her down.

'The master never said that he was expecting visitors,' Elvira stammered. 'It's awful early. He don't get up this early unless it's important.'

Carson touched her chin. 'He's up.'

Elvira stared into his hypnotic eyes. 'He is?'

The last thing she had expected was the long blade of a Bowie knife to be thrust up under her ribcage and twisted. A look of total disbelief washed over the face of Elvira Baker as the taste of blood filled her mouth. Carson moved his gloved hand and covered her face.

Her eyes rolled upward.

Carson pulled his knife free and then wiped the

gore from its blade on his dust coat sleeve. The small female fell heavily on to the floor as Carson slid his knife back into its leather sheath. Within seconds a pool of blood spread out across the tiles. Carson stepped over the body and marched back toward Peters into the living area of the house.

The brutal outlaw had only just reached the foot of the stairs when the Brand boys forcefully dragged their three captives down into the heart of the house. Amos pushed the banker and his wife on to a couch as Luke physically wrestled with the young female.

Carson glared at the older of the brothers. His look said everything without him having to utter a word. Luke Brand released the banker's daughter. She rushed to her parents and threw herself between them.

Petra Hardwick had only just celebrated her fifteenth birthday and as her heart pounded, she began to doubt she would see another. The females whimpered like whipped dogs as they huddled close to the night-gowned Hardwick.

Mustering every scrap of his resolve, the banker stared at the five heavily armed intruders and shook his fist at them.

'This is an outrage,' he boomed. 'I'll have you locked up for this.'

Carson shook his head and strode to a table. He opened a fine silver box and withdrew a fine cigar. He sniffed it and then bit off its tip and placed it between his teeth.

'Keep your voice down, Hardwick,' the leader of the devilish men said as he scratched a match across the highly polished table top. 'We've got a little business to do and then we'll be out of your hair.'

Beth Hardwick looked at her husband. 'Do you know these animals, Stan?'

'I've never met them before.' The banker shrugged.

'But he says you have business to do,' she added.

'Don't go burning his ears, ma'am,' Carson interrupted as he exhaled a long line of grey smoke at the floor. 'Stan don't know anything about the business we've got to do. This is kinda like a surprise.'

The three members of the Hardwick clan sat in their night clothes and watched the merciless outlaw as he savoured the fine cigar and paced around the living room.

Hardwick leaned forward.

'What's all this about?' Hardwick raged before Peters stepped aside and allowed the banker to see the body of the innocent cook. Hardwick gasped as his wife and daughter buried their faces in their hands. The banker stared at the pitiful corpse and then looked in terror at the five dust-caked men who had invaded his home. 'You've killed Elvira. Why?'

Carson grinned. 'I figured it would hone your attention, Hardwick. I reckon I was right. You sure look attentive to me, *amigo*.'

The distraught banker went to stand but Jeff Kane pushed him back on to the couch. Beth clutched his arm to prevent him from attempting to rise again.

'They've killed Elvira, Stan,' she whispered into his ear. 'Don't give them an excuse to do the same to you.'

Hardwick patted her hand. 'You're right, Beth.'

Carson inhaled on the fine cigar and then stared down into the banker's eyes. He pulled the Havana from his mouth and pointed at the overweight man.

'Your woman got sense, Hardwick,' he growled. 'Listen to her and you'll live to see another sunrise.'

The banker gulped. 'What do you want? I don't keep any cash here. My money is in the bank just like everyone else's.'

Carson stepped closer. 'I know that. I also know that you own that big red brick structure down yonder. Nobody can question you coming and going, can they?'

'I don't understand.' Hardwick frowned. 'What exactly are you talking about? Of course I can come and go to the bank. I have the only key.'

Carson screwed up his eyes.

'Then that's exactly what you're gonna do.'

Hardwick started to understand the outlaw. 'You want me to get you into the bank safely?'

Carson leaned over and blew smoke into the face of the banker and then grinned. 'Damn right. Me and my boys don't need to bust into that building if you got the only key. Right?'

Hardwick nodded in agreement. 'Correct.'

Bill Carson sat on the arm of the couch.

'First you're gonna go get dressed and then you, me and a couple of my boys are gonna go visit your bank,' the outlaw announced before patting Hardwick on the back.

Hardwick clutched his wife and child as close to him as he could. He could not stop himself shaking as the acrid aroma of cigar smoke and sweat-soiled clothes filled his nostrils.

'What about Beth and Petra?' the banker croaked. 'If I do what you want, you shall not harm them. Do you promise?'

Carson stood and swung on his heels to face the terrified trio. He laughed at them and then grabbed Hardwick's side whiskers and dragged the banker to his feet. The lethal outlaw pulled him close. So close that the stout banker could feel the heat of the cigar in Carson's gritted teeth burning his cheek.

'Your womenfolk will be fine as long as you obey my orders and don't get smart,' Carson said quietly.

'It don't pay getting smart with Bill, mister,' Poke Peters told the wealthy banker. 'Believe me. If you try to cross Bill he'll do things to these gals of yours that you wouldn't believe.'

Hardwick nodded. 'I'll do anything as long as you do not harm my wife and daughter.'

Carson released his grip and pointed to Amos Brand. 'Take this varmint to his room and watch him get dressed. Then bring him down here.'

Amos Brand grabbed Hardwick by his nightgown and led him up the staircase as if he were taking a dog for a walk. Carson moved slowly around the couch and stared down at the two females. He then paused above the younger female.

She was a cut above the females that the outlaw leader usually encountered. Even her youth could not hide her beauty from the ruthless Carson. Young Petra was like a rose just starting to bloom.

Petrified by his spine-chilling attention, she buried her head into the comforting arms of her equally concerned mother and started to sob as fear overwhelmed her. 'I'm afraid, Mother. Make them go away.'

Yet no matter how much she wanted to comply with her daughter's request, Beth knew it was beyond her abilities. There was no way any of the determined outlaws would listen to her pleas. They encircled the couch like a pack of ravenous hounds.

She looked up at Carson. 'Please stop staring at my daughter. Can't you see she's frightened of you?'

Carson pulled the cigar from his lips, glanced around the faces of his hired help and grinned.

'She's mighty smart, ma'am,' he said coldly. 'If I was in her shoes I reckon I'd be scared too.'

'Why?' the older female asked naively.

Carson pointed at the body of Elvira and smirked. 'That's why you both oughta be mighty scared, ma'am. I can get real dangerous when folks don't do what I tell them.'

Beth Hardwick's expression suddenly changed as her eyes focused on the pitiful sight of the dead female. She gently squeezed her daughter's shoulders and looked directly at Carson as he puffed on his cigar.

'But you promised my husband that as long as he did everything you tell him to do, we'd not be harmed.'

Carson raised his eyebrows and poked his thumbs into his gun belt.

'You'd best pray that I ain't lying, ma'am,' he drawled.

TWO

The main thoroughfare of Fargo slowly warmed as the long shadows gave way to the creeping sunlight. It was still early as acting sheriff Charlie Summers slowly made his way through the streets of Fargo toward the office he had occupied since Sheriff Ben Lomax had taken his deputies, Kid Palomino and Red Rivers to nearby Cooperville to attend a trial at the county seat. All three of Fargo's lawmen were witnesses for the prosecution and had to attend to ensure the guilty party did not get away with murder.

In the meantime Charlie Summers was in charge of the normally sleepy town. The yawning old lawman had been retired more than five years and yet his knowledge was still required by the citizens of Fargo. Summers knew that he was well beyond his best but the quiet town seldom had any real trouble that called for his once formidable prowess. Standing in for Lomax was an easy way to make a few much-needed dollars to supplement his meagre pension.

Fargo was seemingly its usual self. A couple of dogs chased their tails as Summers crossed the empty street. He pulled his battered old timepiece from his vest pocket and checked it. It was still early. Real early. He nodded to himself as he climbed the three steps up to the boardwalk outside the office and paused.

After slipping the dented watch back into his vest pocket, Summers entered the office and raised its window blinds. Sunlight streamed in and the old timer glanced around the twelve-feet square room. He knew that as Lomax and his deputies were due back at any time, he had better clean up.

The old timer blew dust off the rifle rack and then waddled to the cluttered desk. He scratched his neck and pushed his battered hat onto the crown of his balding head.

Charlie stacked the posters into a neat pile and then dusted the newly exposed section of the desk. He paused and yawned again before looking at the stove. He moved to it and opened its iron jaws. He looked in and placed a few crumpled posters into the void. Then he picked up the last of the kindling on to the paper and struck a match. As the paper caught alight and started to envelope the kindling he added more wood until he was happy that he had a fire going.

'That should do it.' Summers clapped his hands together and closed the stove door. He then ladled some water from a bucket into the blackened coffee pot and added a handful of coffee beans. He closed the lid and placed the pot on the stove's flat top. 'Reckon that coffee should be ready in about an hour or so.'

Old Charlie sighed. Nowadays he found that even the slightest effort left him breathless. He squinted out into the quiet street and then returned his attention to the desk. The chair looked very welcoming but the veteran lawman knew that if he sat down he would sleep until noon. He straightened his loose gun belt and rubbed his whiskers.

'Hell, that's enough hard work,' the elderly man reassured himself before walking out on to the boardwalk and resting his bones on the weathered chair. The gentle breeze which looped under the porch overhang was just enough to keep Charlie awake. He pulled out his pipe, tapped it against his boot leather and then started to fill its bowl with tobacco. A solitary buckboard quietly turned the corner and made its way to the feed store.

Summers acknowledged the wave of the driver and then looked down at his pipe. He used his thumb to push the tobacco down into the bowl and then closed the pouch and returned it to his shirt pocket.

'I sure hope Ben and the boys get back today,' he muttered before striking a match along the side of his pants leg and placing it above the bowl. He sucked a few times on the pipe stem and watched as the flame disappeared into the bowl. As smoke filled his mouth he tossed the match at the street and slowly closed his eyes. 'This job is plumb tuckering.'

As the old timer rested, two hundred yards away Bill Carson escorted the terrified banker into the main street and toward the impenetrable red brick edifice. Amos Brand and Poke Peters walked a couple of yards behind the odd pair. Hardwick was wearing his usual hand tailored suit and brown derby. The affluent banker was in total contrast to the three men escorting him in their trail-weary dust coats.

If there had been anyone on the street they might have noticed that the men beside Hardwick were carrying empty saddle-bags across their shoulders. They might have also noticed that the stranger beside him had a firm grip on the elbow of the pale-faced banker. Carson was steering the portly man to the bank to make a hefty withdrawal.

'You'll never get away with this,' Hardwick said as they closed in on the bank.

'Just keep walking and remember that Luke and Jeff are back with your good lady and handsome daughter, Stan,' Carson muttered. 'If there's any trouble, they'll snuff out them gals' candles permanently.

'Savvy?'

The banker nodded.

As Carson helped the banker turn the corner into the main street his eyes darted across the dozens of shuttered store fronts. Barely any of the businesses were open at this ungodly hour and the infamous outlaw knew it. Carson glanced back at Peters and Brand.

'Keep alert, boys,' he commanded.

The outlaws both nodded in reply.

'This is crazy,' Hardwick whispered to his chaperone. 'It'll never work. Folks in Fargo will figure out what's happening and stop you.'

Carson tightened his grip on the elbow of his walking companion. 'You'd better pray that they don't start poking their snouts into this, Hardwick. Just do as I tell you and everything will be OK.'

Even though the banker was probably the wealthiest man in Fargo, there was nothing more precious to him than his wife and child. He would willingly give everything he owned to prevent Beth and Petra suffering the same fate as had befallen Elvira. As the four men trooped to the bank, the terrified and confused banker glanced upward at the church spire that loomed over the far smaller structures at the far end of Fargo. His heart raced. Hardwick had seldom entered the whitewashed church at the end of town but as he and his escorts drew closer to the towering red brick edifice, he began to silently pray.

THREE

The key which opened the reinforced door was returned to the pocket of the banker as Hardwick turned its handle and led his three companions into the dark interior of the bank. Banks of such impressive dimensions were a rarity in this region and none of the men with Hardwick had ever entered such a structure before.

Carson secured the door behind them and then placed his left hand upon Hardwick's shoulder. He leaned down to the far shorter man and growled into his ear.

'You told me that there's a night guard in here, Stan,' he started as his eyes flashed through the unlit depths of the bank. 'Where is he?'

Hardwick felt his heart pound inside his starched shirt as he slowly raised his shaking hand and pointed to their right. All three of the outlaws looked beyond the polished stone pillars to a door set in the corner. The door was totally in sympathy with the rest of the handsome bank. Even in the darkness Carson and his fellow wanted men could see the brass fittings.

'That's his room,' Hardwick stammered as he rubbed the sweat from his features. 'He stays in that room throughout the night and only patrols the bank every hour until the tellers arrive.'

Carson pulled out his pocket watch and checked the time. He showed the timepiece to the banker.

'When does he venture out?' he asked.

'Any moment now,' the banker replied.

Bill Carson returned his watch to his vest, inhaled and then nodded to himself. He looked at Peters and Brand in turn as he drew one of his Remingtons. He cocked the weapon's hammer until it locked into position and pointed to both sides of the door.

'We don't want any shooting,' he hissed at his men. 'Take up positions to either side of the door and I'll try to lure that guard out here. When he comes out, kill him.'

Hardwick gasped in horror. 'No. You can't just kill him.'

Carson pressed the barrel of his gun into the neck of the distraught banker. 'We can and that's what we'll do. Remember, if you wanna see that family of yours again, just keep quiet. Savvy?'

Any concern for the guard evaporated as he thought of his womenfolk. He steadied himself and nodded. 'OK. I'll keep quiet.'

Carson glanced up as both Peters and Brand took up positions to either side of the door. They both waved at Carson who started to push the banker toward the dark-stained door. When both men were ten feet away, Carson halted Hardwick and stepped behind him. He pressed the gun barrel into the base of Hardwick's spine and crouched slightly.

There were no lights burning within the bank. Only gaps around its high windows cast any light into the interior. Spindly shafts of sunlight filtered down into the vast belly of the building.

Even so, Carson did not want the guard to catch a glimpse of him as he hid behind the stocky banker's figure. He gently struck Hardwick in the back with his .45 and hissed.

'Call him,' Carson snarled.

Even knowing that he was about to lure the guard to his death, Hardwick mustered up every scrap of his resolve and called out.

'This is Hardwick, Elias,' he said. 'I've had to come in early to sort out a few things before we open.'

He heard the bolt being slid behind the door and then watched as the trusting man ventured out toward him. 'Howdy, Mr Hardwick. I'm sure glad you warned me that you was in here early.'

Hardwick watched helplessly as both Brand and Peters pounced on the unsuspecting man. The knives in their hands caught the rays of the filtered sunlight as they were plunged into the guard. Bright flashes danced off the polished interior of the bank's fittings.

The banker lowered his head as Brand grabbed the boots of the lifeless man and hauled him back into the small room where he had happily sat less than sixty seconds earlier.

Carson pushed Hardwick toward the pool of blood that trailed the body to where it was deposited. The leader of the merciless trio walked around the banker and patted both men on their shoulders.

'You done good, boys,' he exclaimed before holstering his gun and returning his eyes to the shaking banker. He pointed a finger at Hardwick. 'Now it's your turn to make good our bargain, Stan boy.'

Hardwick looked up. He was filled with shame for his part in the brutal murder of the guard and yet knew that like all family men, he had no choice. He had to comply.

'Follow me,' he said in a faltering voice as he started walking toward the strong room behind the line of teller windows. 'I'll take you to the vault.'

Bill Carson gritted his teeth and pushed the banker violently between his shoulders.

'Lead the way, Stan,' he drawled. 'Lead the way.'

FOUR

The street was getting warmer as the sun slowly crept higher into the morning sky. Charlie Summers had drifted into a deep sleep outside the sheriff's office as he sat stretched out on the old wooden chair beneath the porch overhang. Normally the retired lawman would have continued to snore for more than another hour but as the street grew busier, the noise wrestled him out of his dreams.

For a moment the ancient lawman had no idea where he was or how long he had been there. Summers opened his eyes and pushed the brim of his battered old hat off his eyes and squinted at a buckboard as it squeaked along the street. There were a few of the town's womenfolk strolling toward the heart of Fargo with baskets hanging over their arms and brightly coloured parasols resting upon their shoulders.

The elderly lawman blinked several times to clear his eyes and then sat upright. He pulled the pipe from his mouth and spat at the boardwalk.

'That wagon sure needs oiling,' he grumbled as he vainly sucked and blew into the stem of the pipe trying to rekindle it. As was usual with even the finest of tobaccos, it had stopped burning. Old Charlie gave the pipe bowl a frustrated look and then thrust it into his vest pocket.

He was about to stretch his ancient bones when he caught sight of two dusty horsemen moving slowly through the heat haze. Charlie rubbed his tired eyes and stood as he vainly tried to focus clearly on the riders.

'Now who in tarnation are them varmints?' he asked himself cautiously as he rested the palm of his hand on the gun in its holster. 'Whoever they are they sure don't look peaceable.'

Charlie raised a thin arm, rested the palm of his hand on the porch upright and rubbed his old eyes again. 'Why in hell is everyone so blurred nowadays?'

The words had barely had time to leave his lips when he noticed that the riders had tugged on their long leathers and were headed in his direction.

'Ah, hell,' Charlie cursed and stared at the shimmering horsemen. 'They're heading here.'

Just as Charlie thought, the riders were indeed guiding their mounts toward the sheriff's office and the old man who was watching them. Summers nervously scratched his whiskered chin and then polished the tin star he wore with his shirt cuff. He dropped his hand until his finger curled around the holstered trigger of his trusty .44.

Summoning every last ounce of his courage, Charlie walked down the boardwalk until he was at the edge of the porch. He held his hand up in an attempt to stop the riders.

'Hold on there, boys,' Charlie said in his deepest and most authoritative of tones. 'Who are you and how come you're in Fargo?'

The horse continued on toward the valiant old timer. Then the riders drew rein and halted beside the hitching rail.

'Sorry to wake you, Charlie,' one of the horsemen chuckled as he swung his leg over his cantle and lowered himself to the ground.

'Which one of you varmints said that?' Charlie Summers took another step and then grabbed hold of the wooden upright as one of his boots overstepped the edge of the boardwalk.

'Careful there, Charlie,' the youthful voice of the rider sat astride the high-shouldered palomino stallion said before adding, 'You don't wanna break that scrawny neck of yours, do you?'

Summers looked at Red Rivers as he looped his reins over the hitching pole and secured it. He then looked up at the rider straddling the stallion. A smile erupted on the old timer's face.

'I knew it was you boys, Kid,' he chortled. 'I knew it was you boys all the time.'

'No you didn't, Charlie,' Red Rivers argued. 'You thought we were a couple of desperadoes ready to start shooting up the town.'

Summers looked at Red as he stepped up beside him.

'The sun was in my eyes, Red boy. I'd have figured out who you was soon enough.' He shrugged.

'Sure you would.' Kid Palomino smiled as he slid to the ground beside his mount. He tied his long leathers to the twisted pole beside Red's quarter horse and then rested his knuckles on his gun grips. He stared up at the two men.

Charlie looked uneasy at the handsome young deputy. He turned to Red. 'What's the Kid looking at, Red boy?'

'He's looking at you.' Red replied.

'I know that,' Charlie croaked, 'but why?'

Red shook his head. 'Damned if I know.'

'I'll tell you why I'm looking at you, Charlie.' Palomino stepped up on to the boardwalk and placed a hand on the skinny shoulder of the retired sheriff. 'I'm plumb thirsty, Charlie. I sure hope you've got the coffee brewing.'

The eyes of the older man sparkled. 'You like my coffee, Kid?'

'I sure do.' Palomino walked with his two companions into the office. Steam was rising from the blackened pot on top of the pot-belly stove. 'Besides it's too early to go to the café and get a decent cup.'

Summers rustled up three tin cups and spread them out on the desk. He stared at the pot and scratched his beard. 'I must have bin asleep longer than I figured.'

Red glanced at the wall clock. 'It's twenty after eight.'

'Holy crackers,' Old Charlie gasped as he used a cloth to pick up the coffee pot off the stove top. 'Time sure does fly.'

'I guess it flies even faster when you're getting some shuteye,' the Kid remarked as he watched all three cups being filled.

Charlie started to chuckle. 'Reckon it does.'

Palomino picked up a tin cup and went to the open door and leaned a shoulder against the frame. As he raised the cup to his lips something at the far end of the street caught his attention.

'What did you say the time was, Red?' he asked as

he stared through the steam of his beverage.

'I said that it's twenty after eight, Kid,' Red repeated as he took a mouthful of coffee and swallowed. 'Why'd you ask?'

Palomino glanced at the two lawmen and then returned his eyes to what had intrigued him along the street. 'What time does Hardwick open that big old bank of his?'

Charlie Summers shook his head and glanced at Palomino.

'You know perfectly well that Stan never opens the bank before ten in the morning, Kid.' Charlie sighed. 'What you asking such a dumb question for?'

Palomino downed his coffee and then tossed the empty cup at his pals. Red caught the tin cup and placed it down on the desk.

'What's eating you, Palomino?' Red asked.

Kid Palomino looked at his companions. 'If Hardwick doesn't open up his bank until ten in the morning, what's he doing with three *hombres* coming out of the place right now?'

'You're imagining things, Kid,' Summers scoffed.

'Hell, I've never seen that rich old dude at this time of the morning, Palomino,' Red agreed with the elderly Summers. 'Bankers don't get up early like regular folks.'

Kid Palomino tilted his head. 'Well he's up and

walking this morning. Come take a looksee if you don't believe me.'

Intrigued by Palomino's insistence, Red and Charlie moved to the side of the younger lawman and watched as the four men made their way from the red brick edifice and started heading back toward the corner on their way to Hardwick's house.

'Ain't that Hardwick?' Palomino asked.

'It sure is and he ain't on his lonesome,' Red agreed.

Palomino pushed the brim of his Stetson back. 'I don't like the look of them three *hombres* with him. They're packing too much iron for my liking.'

'You're right,' Red agreed as he scratched his cheek thoughtfully. 'They're also carrying saddle-bags, Kid.'

'Mighty swollen saddle-bags by the looks of them, Red,' Palomino added before raising his eyebrows. 'Now what do you reckon them three *hombres* got in them bags?'

Charlie looked at Red and Palomino in turn. 'I can't see a damn thing, boys. Are you sure that's Stan Hardwick?'

'We're sure, Charlie,' Red nodded.

'Unlock the rifle rack and get me a Winchester, old timer,' the Kid told Summers.

Summers nodded. 'Sure enough, Kid.'

As the old man scooped a bunch of keys off the desk and moved to the padlock dangling from the line of secured rifles, Red glanced at him.

'You'd best get me one as well, Charlie,' he said.

'Make sure they're loaded, Charlie,' Palomino added. 'I'd hate to confront them *hombres* with empty guns.'

Old Charlie pulled a few repeating rifles off the rack and checked them in turn. The rifles' magazines were all fully loaded.

'Hurry up, Charlie,' Palomino urged. 'They've turned the corner. We can't see them anymore.'

'I couldn't even see them when they was there,' Summers muttered as he staggered to the pair of deputies with three repeating rifles in his thin arms. Palomino took one as Red lifted another. Both men cranked the weapons' mechanisms.

'What's the other rifle for, Charlie?' Palomino asked.

An impish smile etched the whiskered face as the veteran lawman cranked the hand guard of the third Winchester sending a spent casing over his shoulder.

'This'uns for me, Kid,' he winked.

Palomino smiled at the feisty old man.

'C'mon,' he told them. 'Let's go find out what Hardwick and them *hombres* are up to.'

FIVE

No riverboat gambler could have looked more the part, but the man in the frilly shirt with its black lace tie hanging down to the silk vest was not what he appeared to be. The white wide-brimmed hat and tailored blue frock coat seemed to scream out that this was a man who made his living at the gaming tables but it was all a well-devised illusion. He was not what he pretended to be.

Everything about him was calculated to deceive, for in reality the gambler was probably one of the most dangerous of people who had ever existed.

Danby Deacon had never done an honest day's work in his entire forty-nine years of existence. Men like Deacon had always shunned anything remotely resembling work and found other ways to make their living. He exercised his brain power rather than his muscles.

Although Deacon was never close to the brutal activities he had masterminded, he was never too far away. As long as there was a telegraph office close, Deacon would keep in touch with his underlings.

Deacon had come a long way from the shady streets of his native New York. They had helped to sharpen his skills as a con artist and trickster. Once he realized that he could make more money by planning jobs for others, he had ventured out into the quickly growing West. As towns sprang up and spread like cancers across the vast land, Deacon was usually there.

To most he was just another gambler.

In reality he was something far more lethal. For Deacon had the knack of listening while others talked. When folks talked, they betrayed themselves and others. They allowed men of an unscrupulous nature to work out what was the truth and what was exaggeration.

Years of practice had made him the best there was at his hideous profession. As he silently played cards he absorbed everything his fellow gamblers said.

Deacon would discover names, addresses and anything else he thought vital to perfecting his plan. Then he would relay the details to the ruthless outlaws who relied upon his detailed information in order to execute his outrageous plan with the least amount of opposition.

It had worked perfectly for years.

Yet even though the meticulous mastermind had made both Bill Carson and himself wealthy men, they had never actually met. Deacon preferred it that way. He knew that those who seek glory seldom live long enough to actually enjoy the fruits of their labours. Yet although Carson knew nothing about Deacon apart from calling him 'the Deacon', the vastly more intelligent Deacon knew everything there was to know about his cohort.

Every scrap of information concerning the notorious outlaw was branded into Deacon's memory. The wild streets of his youth had taught him that knowledge was power and when you were dealing with men like Carson, you needed to be in total control.

Deacon would mail letters to pre-arranged places for Carson to read and obey. All other messages between the two men were sent via the telegraph.

That had proven to be a lucrative arrangement for both parties and meant that Deacon was always well away from the action when it erupted.

For years he had provided some of the deadliest outlaws with vital information that they then used. It was Deacon who had weighed up the banker Stanley Hardwick and discovered what made him tick. He had passed this information on to Bill Carson for a share of the takings the outlaw could get from the banker's seemingly impregnable establishment.

Deacon had passed through Fargo a week earlier and visited every saloon and gambling house in the town until he had gathered all the information he needed.

His habit of quietly playing poker had once again paid dividends. Men talked freely as they drank whiskey and won hand after hand to Deacon. Their excitement only loosened their tongues more as the card games stretched on into the night and their stacks of gaming chips grew taller and taller.

It was exactly the same in every town Deacon visited.

Deacon had lost count how many times he had repeated the beneficial act. And none of them had ever realized that they were being used. All they could see was the money they were winning from the stranger in their midst.

Deacon would be gracious and bow out when he had discovered everything he wanted to know, and then depart. The victorious gamblers would mock him with no idea that they had just had their mutual knowledge stripped by the best trickster any of them would ever meet.

Satisfied that he had discovered every minute detail concerning the owner of the impressive red brick bank, Deacon had taken the next stagecoach from Fargo and travelled to where he had instructed Carson to wire him.

The small town of Cherokee Springs sat at the very edge of an unnamed desert. It was one of those sun-bleached places that few men ever visited unless they had reason to hole up for a while. Even the law shied away from making the perilous trip across the arid terrain to Cherokee Springs.

Deacon though, knew that it was perfect for his needs. It was an ideal spot to wait for Carson and his hirelings to rob the bank at Fargo. Deacon had alighted from the stagecoach a few days before and rented the best room in the ramshackle hotel.

As agreed, he would send meaningless telegraph wires to Carson in the next town along the stagecoach route and wait for the reply that would confirm the job had done his bidding for him.

Cherokee Springs was twenty hard-bitten miles from Dry Gulch. Deacon was a man who favoured good cigars and even better whiskey. The solitary saloon in the small settlement provided both as well as female company.

Danby Deacon would willingly indulge heavily in

all the temptations the town offered as he waited for news that Carson had fulfilled his part of the bargain.

Once he had been paid, he would set off for the next large town and start his methodical work all over again. Deacon knew that Bill Carson was a dangerous outlaw who seldom shared out the spoils of his endeavours with any of the numerous men he hired. Only Deacon had always received his cut of the take because even Carson realized that the man who he had never seen was invaluable.

Before responding to a mysterious message from Deacon, years earlier, Carson had been fortunate to survive his attempts at train and bank robbery.

Although he hated to admit it, Carson knew that he could not plan his jobs as masterly as his unknown benefactor. He needed the mysterious Deacon.

They both knew it.

As he waited in Cherokee Springs, Deacon rested his freshly shaven chin on the heaving bosom of one of the town's working girls who straddled his lap. He took a sip of whiskey and savoured its warming glow as it burned a trail down into his gullet.

'What do you do, Danby?' the soiled dove asked as she pressed her heaving flesh into his welcoming face. 'I mean, what do you do for a job?'

There was a long silence as the man who masqueraded as a common gambler considered the question. Her heavily scented flesh filled his flared nostrils as his eyes darted at her powdered face. A wry smile etched his features as her finger curled his side-whiskers. Deacon looked her straight in the eyes and offered her a tumbler of his fine whiskey. She downed the hard liquor with expertise.

'I think and wait, honey-child,' he sighed.

'What do you think and wait for, Danby darling?' she purred into his ear as she nibbled upon it.

'Money, honey-child,' he answered. 'I think about money.'

SIX

A scattering of trees flanked both sides of the street on the way to the half-hidden lane that led to where the banker's elegant residence stood. Bill Carson and his two cohorts were laden down under the weight of their fully filled saddle-bags as they strode through the leafy enclave. With every stride the wanted men kept pushing Hardwick forward as their eyes darted at the neighbouring buildings for any sign of impending trouble.

They need not have troubled themselves. It was still early and the wealthy people who lived in this small section of Fargo did not rise at this ungodly hour.

The four men closed in on the end structure and moved to the rear of the building. Steam rose from their four horses as they walked past them and entered the banker's home.

A blood-chilling sound met their ears as they crossed the tiled floor of the kitchen. It was the noise that signals the final gasps of life as they succumb to death.

The pitiful body of the maid was still exactly where they had left it. The pool of blood had grown larger and stickier since Carson had ended Elvira's existence. Yet it was not the sight of the brutally murdered female that had drawn the banker's attention. It was what had happened to his womenfolk that enraged the normally peaceful man. Hardwick clenched both his fists in helpless fury when he saw what had occurred in his absence.

His wife and daughter had been brutally assaulted and lay where the two outlaws had left them. Hardwick stared in horror at the bruised throats of both females as they draped the long couch lifelessly.

They looked like porcelain dolls. Every scrap of life and been mercilessly ripped from them. Dignity had been replaced by shock on their dead faces.

'What have you done?' The banker shouted at the satisfied pair. 'What have you done?'

The outlaws glared at the banker as they tucked their shirts back into their belts and then started to laugh at the outraged man.

'Quit belly-aching,' Brand spat at the stunned banker in amusement. 'We give them what they needed.'

'Don't worry, Beth,' Hardwick called to his spouse.

Carson leaned over the shorter man and hissed like a rattler into Hardwick's ear. 'She can't hear you, Stan. Neither of your ladies can hear nothing but the sound of harps now.'

'They're not dead,' the banker vainly insisted. 'They can't be dead.'

'They're dead OK.' Brand laughed as he moved toward the colourless face of the banker. 'Me and Kane seen to that after them gals obliged us.'

'You filthy animals!' The banker went to rush at the mocking pair when he felt the full force of Carson's gun hit the back of his head. Suddenly his eyes only saw a white flashing light. He stumbled and then toppled on to the boards. His face crashed into the floor as he sank into a bottomless pit of total oblivion.

Carson holstered his gun. The infamous outlaw shook his head in anger and glared at Kane and Brand. 'You shouldn't have done that, boys. Them females were screaming fit to burst when we showed up.'

Kane adjusted his gun-belt. 'We couldn't kill them

before we had our fun, could we?'

'Why not?' Carson spat and paced around the room and looked out from behind the heavily draped window. 'You're lucky by the looks of it. It don't seem that their howling woke up the neighbours.'

'What if they did wake anybody up?' Brand snarled.

Carson glanced at Brand and pointed a finger at the outlaw.

'Screaming women might have brought unwanted attention here. That weren't in my plans.'

Peters nodded in agreement. 'Bill's right. We need to ride out of Fargo without anybody even knowing we were ever here in the first place. Ain't that right, Bill?'

'Yep, that's right, Poke,' Carson agreed.

Carson stepped over the unconscious banker and looked at the sight of his two hired men as they buttoned up their pants and shirts. His icy stare wiped the satisfied smirks from their rugged faces.

Peters cleared his throat. 'Ain't it time for us to be headed out of here, Bill? We got as much money as we can carry and if we high-tail it now, we'll be long gone before anybody figures that anything's wrong.'

Carson spat as he helped himself to a handful of the banker's cigars, pocketed all but one and struck a match. As its flame ignited the fine Havana he nodded at Peters.

'You're right, Poke,' he answered before pulling his knife from its scabbard and staring at the three figures scattered around the living room.

Slowly Carson removed the heavy saddle-bag from his shoulder and rested the swollen satchels on the edge of the couch. Without uttering a word the merciless leader of the gang stepped to where the bodies of the women were draped and then slid the honed blade across their bruised throats. He then straightened up and wiped the gore from the gleaming blade as he walked across the room to where both Kane and Brand stood.

'Why'd you do that, Bill?' Kane asked. 'They were both dead. They didn't need their throats cut.'

Faster than either of the rugged outlaws had ever seen anyone move before, Carson ran the deadly Bowie knife under their chins. They gulped in terror.

'I was just making sure they were dead and not just play-acting, boys,' Carson laughed as he looked down at the unconscious banker.

Then from behind his wide shoulders he heard the voice of the other Brand brother.

'Quit waving that cutlass around, Bill,' he said.

Carson paused and stared at the nervy outlaw.

'You talking to me, boy?'

'I sure am,' the younger Brand dragged the saddle-bags from his shoulder and rested his hand on his holstered gun. 'You better not be thinking of sticking my brother with that blade. I'll kill you if you do.'

The half-closed eyes of Carson fixed on Brand's sibling and shook his head. 'Don't even think about drawing that hog-leg, boy.'

'If you stick my brother with that cutlass I'll draw, Bill,' Brand warned. 'Don't make me draw.'

Bill Carson smiled. It was the sickly smile of a man who knew exactly how fast he was and feared no one. He shook his head and exhaled a long line of grey smoke.

'Easy, I ain't gonna kill your brother, boy.' Carson muttered a fraction of a heartbeat before he stepped away from the pair and loomed over Hardwick's prostrate body. His eyes darted between the banker and the riled Brand brother. 'Now quit threatening me before I forget whose side you're on.'

The outlaw relaxed and glanced back at Peters. He shrugged and then rubbed his rugged features. 'That was close.'

'You don't know how close, Brand.' Peters agreed as he watched Carson look down at the stunned banker as he quietly knelt over Hardwick.

With another swift slash of the knife, Carson ruthlessly dispatched the banker. He stood and looked at the blood spilling out over the floor and smiled. Then he wiped the bloody blade on his sleeve, and stepped back over the corpse and moved to his saddle-bags. He plucked them up and tossed them into the hands of Peters.

'Now we're ready to depart this damn town,' he grunted as his cruel eyes surveyed the outrage. 'We're done here.'

The outlaws gathered around their leader as he savoured the expensive cigar between his teeth. None of the band could figure out Carson. He was like a stick of dynamite with its fuse lit. The trouble was they had no idea how long his fuse actually was.

'Was you figuring on bedding either of them females, Bill?' Kane wondered as he pulled on his dust coat again.

'Nope.' Carson waved the fine Havana around and said dryly, 'I have my fun when the killing and robbing is done and dusted. You should do the same if'n you intend staying alive long enough to spend your share of the loot.'

Peters looked anxious to leave. 'Let's get out of here, Bill. I got me a real bad feeling about this town.'

'OK,' Carson blew smoke into Brand's face before

turning and staring at Kane. 'Ready the horses, boy.'

Kane did not argue. He ran from the room and headed out into the back yard.

There was no talking in the large living room for a few moments as Carson walked thoughtfully around the banker. He stared down at the gash across the back of Hardwick's scalp and the pool of blood which now encircled the head.

'You, Luke and Amos take the saddle-bags out to the horses,' he told Poke Peters through cigar smoke. 'Tie all three of the saddle-bags to my horse, Poke. Two to the cantle and one across the saddle horn.'

'You want me to laden your horse down with all of the saddle-bags, Bill?' Peters checked as he picked the hefty bags off the floor and the Brand siblings did the same. 'These bags are a real load for one horse.'

'You heard me, Poke,' he drawled before eyeing them all in turn and then striding toward the back door. 'Strap all three of them saddle-bags to my horse.'

The outlaws trailed Carson out into the bright yard.

'Have you checked the cinch straps?' Carson asked Kane.

Kane nodded. 'Yep, I checked them all.'

Bill Carson tightened his gloves over his knuckles and then pulled the cigar from his lips. He tossed the spent smoke aside, grabbed his long leathers and poked his boot into the stirrup.

'Mount up, boys,' he hissed as he looped his leg over the saddle and then gathered up his reins. 'We'll be long gone before anyone knows we were ever here.'

'Where we headed, Bill?' Peters asked as he mounted his high-shouldered gelding.

'We're off to a place call Dry Gulch, Poke,' Carson replied before backing his mount away from the large house.

'Dry Gulch?' Amos Brand repeated. 'What in tarnation are we headed there for? That's in the middle of the desert, ain't it?'

Carson nodded and then pulled the brim of his Stetson down to shield his eyes. 'Yep, it sure is.'

'But how come we're going there?' Kane wondered as he swung his horse around.

'Coz the Deacon told me to go there,' Carson answered dryly. 'And I always listen to the Deacon.'

'How come?' Kane asked. 'Is he the boss?'

'Nope, he's the brains,' Carson corrected.

The five horsemen steered their mounts out from the yard into the blazing sunlight.

SEVEN

The shadows were getting shorter with every beat of Kid Palomino's heart as he led Red and Charlie across the wide main street and up an alley. It was hot as the bowels of hell and getting hotter. The young deputy knew that the winding alley cut through the numerous wooden and brick structures and led to the side street. Shafts of blinding sunlight burned down on to the exposed confines with a merciless determination that Palomino had grown used to in this part of Fargo.

He pulled the brim of his hat down to shield his face from the hot rays he knew could strip skin from bone. The heat within the alley grew more intense. Sweat ran freely from every pore in his tall frame. He was soaked as though he had been caught in a downpour of rain. Yet no rain tasted like the beads of sweat that negotiated his chiselled features and found his lips.

Palomino licked the salty residue from his lips and glanced back to his fellow lawmen as they tried to keep pace with his long, lean legs.

The Kid rested against a brick wall at the end of the alley, cocked the Winchester and stared out into the blazing street.

By his calculations Hardwick and his three heavily laden companions would have to pass this way in a few moments. As he waited Red and the old timer caught up with him.

'Why'd you stop, Palomino?' Charlie asked as he bent double and sucked in air. 'The way you was moving I figured you wouldn't stop until you got the drop on them fellas.'

Palomino dried his face with his shirt sleeve and screwed up his eyes against the sun which reflected off the white sand at their feet.

'I seen old Hardwick and them strangers turn the corner near the bank,' the Kid sighed heavily. 'I figured they were headed this way.'

'You reckoning on stopping them *hombres* in their tracks, Kid?' Red said as he clutched the repeating rifle to his chest in readiness.

Palomino nodded. 'Yep.'

Old Charlie edged out from the corner and

squinted hard into the quiet thoroughfare.

'Are you sure this is the way they was headed, Palomino?' he asked. 'I sure can't see or hear them.'

The face of the young deputy looked long and hard at the old lawman and then pulled him back into the alley. Palomino poked his head around the corner and cautiously stared into the street himself.

Charlie was right. None of the four men they hoped to get the drop on were anywhere to be seen. The Kid returned to the alley and frowned.

'Charlie's right, Red,' the Kid muttered.

'What you talking about?' Red asked Palomino. He had seen the totally baffled look on Palomino's face many times before and it troubled him. He moved closer to his pal. 'You look like a dog that's just lost a bone.'

'I've lost four bones, Red,' Palomino mumbled as he stroked the rifle in his hands thoughtfully. 'Take a look if you don't believe me. They're gone.'

'I mean them galoots ain't there,' Palomino added.

'I told you they weren't there,' Charlie nodded. 'They've up and vanished, Red.'

'They can't be gone.' It seemed impossible to Red as he brushed both his companions aside and carefully peeked around the corner wall into the street. His jaw dropped in utter bewilderment. 'Hell, they are gone.'

'I told you that already,' Charlie nodded.

'Where in tarnation are they?' Red blurted.

Palomino glanced at the sturdy deputy. 'Damned if I know where they are, Red. All I know is that they ain't where they should be.'

Red stared blankly into Palomino's baffled face. 'How could they just disappear like that, Kid? That ain't natural.'

Palomino rubbed the sweat off his mouth.

'I thought I knew this town like the back of my hand but them varmints with old Stan have just up and vanished into thin air,' the Kid said in disbelief. 'That ain't possible.'

'Are you boys sure that you seen old Stan and them tall gun-toting varmints leaving the bank, Kid?' Charlie asked his younger companion.

'What in tarnation are you gabby about?' Red leaned over the skinny star-packer. 'You seen them too, Charlie. We all seen them.'

The ancient lawman shook his head and waved his finger under the nose of the deputy. 'I didn't see 'em.'

'You must have,' Palomino looked at the feisty old timer. 'You was standing right next to us. I seen them and so did Red. You must have seen them, Charlie.'

'Hell, I couldn't even see the bank from the

sheriff's porch, boy,' Charlie admitted, pointing to his eyes. 'Not with these peepers. All I saw was a blur. All I ever see lately is damn blurs.'

Palomino rested his hand on Red's shoulder. 'I know what I saw and I saw Hardwick and three heavily armed galoots toting saddle-bags.'

Red nodded. 'I seen them too, Kid.'

Kid Palomino bit his lip as his mind raced in search of an answer to the puzzle it was wrestling with. 'They headed this way. That's why I chose to use this alleyway as a shortcut. I figured on getting ahead of them.'

Red rubbed his neck and stepped out into the quiet street as his eyes vainly searched every dwelling and store front for a clue as to where the three unknown men and Hardwick might have gone. Finally he shook his head and rested the Winchester barrel against his temple.

'This is plumb loco,' he growled. 'There ain't no stores along this street that open at this ungodly hour, Kid. Them *hombres* must have gone someplace else with Stan.'

'But where did they go, Red?' Palomino wondered as he tucked his rifle under his arm.

Charlie Summers shook his head and started to turn. 'I'm headed back to the office and get me some shuteye, boys. You figure it out and then come and wake me.'

Palomino grabbed the scrawny shoulder of the veteran lawman and pulled him back. 'You ain't going nowhere, Charlie. Not until we find them critters and ask them what they was doing in the bank.'

Charlie looked at the tall deputy. 'Sheriff Lomax will be back soon, Kid. I gotta go and tidy the office before he rides in. That critter is damn fussy, you know.'

Palomino and Red looked at one another and then at the far smaller man. They grinned at the cantankerous old timer.

'You're gonna tidy the office?' Red repeated his words. 'Exactly how are you gonna do that, Charlie?'

Charlie thought for a moment and then wryly smiled. 'I'm gonna mosey on back and dust the office. The sheriff is partial to a good dusting.'

'Sure he is,' Red chuckled.

Palomino released his grip. 'Go on then, Charlie. Go dust the office while me and Red start looking for Stan and them *hombres.*'

Charlie was about to do as he was told when they all three of them heard the muffled sound of hoofs. Palomino glanced at his two pals and looked around them.

'Do you hear that, boys?' Charlie asked.

'I heard that, Charlie,' Red confirmed as he

stepped to the corner and glanced around the empty street. 'I hear horses but where in tarnation are they?'

Kid Palomino bit his lower lip and rested his knuckles on his gun grips. 'Where'd you figure they are?'

The veteran lawman ambled between his two younger companions and squinted hard. Although his eyes could no longer see as they had once done, his hearing was still as sharp as ever. He squinted hard at the mass of trees fifty feet from where they stood. He raised a scrawny finger and pointed.

'Them horses are somewhere over yonder, boys,' he told the deputies. 'I can hear about three or maybe more horses. Can you see them yet?'

Palomino pulled his hat brim down to shield his eyes.

'I reckon you're right, Charlie. It sure sounds like horses walking beyond them trees,' he agreed.

Red shook his head. 'I can't see a thing.'

Palomino frowned.

'Charlie's right, Red,' he said. 'Them horses we can hear are halfway down the street someplace.'

Red slapped his thigh in frustration with himself. 'Damn it all. That's where they built a few real fancy houses for the rich folks, Kid. I plumb forgot about it.'

Before either Palomino or Charlie could reply, Bill Carson led his four hired gunmen out from the confines of the well-hidden alleyway into the side street. As the infamous outlaw turned his head he saw the three star-packers and pulled back on his long leathers. His mount stopped as his four fellow outlaws trailed him into the bright sunshine.

'What you looking at, Bill?' Peters asked as he halted his own horse beside Carson's tall mount.

Carson did not speak. He simply raised a finger and pointed at the three lawmen watching them. The outlaws sat in their saddles and gazed through the shimmering heat haze to where Palomino and his pals were standing.

'Them's lawmen,' Luke Brand spat.

'They're packing repeating rifles, Bill,' Kane added.

'You said they were out of town.' Amos Brand steadied his nervous mount.

Bill Carson shook his head.

'They're meant to be out of town, boys,' he hissed.

Kid Palomino stepped forward. His eyes narrowed as they focused on the lead rider. Carson pulled his reins to his belly and stared along the street at them. The ruthless outlaw had never seen any of the three standing men before but it was not their faces that had drawn his interest.

It was the tin stars pinned to their chests that Carson was looking at. They were gleaming like precious gems across the distance between them. Carson looped the reins around his saddle horn and then slowly placed his hands on his pair of pearl-handled Remingtons.

'What we gonna do, Bill?' Kane asked his merciless leader.

'There's only one thing we can do, Kane,' Carson said in a low whisper as his fingers curled around the holstered guns. 'Lawmen are like Injuns and they say the only good'uns are dead'uns. The same applies to star-packing bastards like them critters.'

Poke Peters moved his horse to the head of Carson's. 'I like your thinking, Bill. Ain't nothing more satisfying than killing lawmen.'

The mind of Kid Palomino was racing like a locomotive under a full head of steam. He focused hard on the lead rider and then realized who he was looking at. He looked to both his companions in turn.

'That's Bill Carson, boys,' Palomino stated confidently as he pulled the Winchester from under his arm and readied it for action. 'I've seen his wanted poster a hundred times over the last few years.'

Before either Red or Charlie could respond to the Kid's statement they noticed the horsemen suddenly swing their mounts violently around to face them. As dust rose from the hoofs of the five animals the air began to crackle with fiery lead as the outlaws suddenly unleashed their arsenal on the trio of lawmen.

Red hot tapers cut through the shimmering haze and whizzed by the law officers. Palomino dragged the old man behind a water trough as Red took refuge in a doorway.

Within a few moments the street became deafening as the outlaws kept firing their guns at them. Chunks of wood were ripped from the rim of the trough and flew up into the air. At the same time the side of the doorframe where Red had taken refuge also began to disintegrate as bullets tore into its lumber.

Red pressed his back against the door. He waited for a brief lull in the vicious attack and then blasted his Winchester at the outlaws. Yet for every shot he managed to fire at Carson and his gang, at least six bullets were returned. Red was trapped and he knew it. Bullets continued to gnaw away at the wall beside Red's shoulder until he was covered in burning sawdust.

Crouching behind the cover of the water trough, Kid Palomino and the startled old timer were also pinned down.

'This is getting serious, Kid,' Charlie piped up.

'I'm starting to get mighty riled.'

Kid patted the veteran lawman on his skinny shoulder.

'Don't get riled, Charlie,' he said from the corner of his mouth. 'I'll try to fend the bastards off.'

The young deputy primed his rifle and then moved around the side of the trough. He fired repeatedly until the Winchester's magazine was empty and then moved back beside Charlie.

'They're still shooting at us, Kid,' the old man sighed and exchanged rifles with his companion. 'Here, use this'un.'

'Thanks, Charlie.' Palomino cranked its mechanism.

Just as he was about to turn and fire another volley of lethal lead at the outlaws he felt a scrawny hand grip his arm. He looked at the whiskered face.

'Try and hit some of them this time,' Charlie said.

'I'll do my best,' the Kid answered as another barrage of bullets ripped into the fabric of the water trough. 'You can reload my rifle for me.'

As the older lawman started to remove bullets from his gunbelt and push them into the rifle's magazine, Palomino turned and rested on both knees. The blinding sun mixed with the ever increasing smoke coming from the outlaw's gun barrels made it tough for even his young eyes to find a target but the

Kid was determined to try.

Flashes of deafening gunfire lit up the eerie street and drilled into the trough as Palomino gripped the Winchester firmly and raised its metal barrel. He focused along the gun sights at the fiery flashes and then fired.

Within seconds bullets came at him from the riders' arsenal of six-shooters. The ground around the trough was peppered with lead. A cloud of choking dust flew up and forced Palomino to retreat to the side of the grumbling old timer.

'You'd best start killing them varmints before they kill us, Kid,' Charlie sniffed.

'I'm trying, old timer.' Palomino rubbed the dust from his face as they felt the trough behind their backs rock under the deadly onslaught.

Charlie raised his bushy eyebrows. 'Try harder.'

Flabbergasted by his elderly pal's attitude, Palomino decided to try harder. He crawled over the skinny legs of the old lawman and immediately started firing the rifle from the opposite corner of the trough.

Shafts of lead criss-crossed the length of the street. The outlaws had the three star-packers trapped and they knew it. Slowly they began to edge their mounts closer to their cornered targets. The entire street was engulfed in red-hot tapers and enough noise to shatter eardrums.

Palomino exhausted his rifle's ammunition and crawled back to Charlie's side. He thrust the smoking rifle into the old timer's hands and grabbed the fully loaded weapon.

Red fired three swift shots from his place of cover. Then he was forced back behind the bullet-ridden wall as every one of the horsemen fired at him.

'Are you OK, Red?' the Kid yelled out above the relentless din of gunfire.

'I think so,' Red gasped as yet another half-dozen shots tore even more of the wooden door frame apart.

'I've had me enough of this, Charlie.' Kid Palomino cranked the hand guard of his rifle and then swiftly swung around and began to empty its venom at the approaching horsemen. 'Now I'm getting darn sore at Carson and his gang.'

Charlie Summers clapped his hands. 'Hallelujah! Now maybe we'll send them bastards to Boot Hill.'

Bullets ripped into the trough that the Kid was shielded behind. Water sprayed up over the defiant deputy as he continued to fire his Winchester at the horsemen.

The toxic mix of gunsmoke and hoof dust did not make the task of hitting any of the targets Palomino had chosen to shoot at any easier. Yet the simple matter that he could not see any of the outlaws did not deter Palomino.

The Kid knew that if you couldn't see the men you were aiming at you looked for the bright flashes their six-guns spewed out. His eyes narrowed as he quickly blasted the Winchester every time they fired their guns.

His lethal accuracy began to pay off. He heard one of Carson's men yelp like a kicked hound.

Red stepped out on to the boardwalk and fired his own rifle into the men masked by choking gunsmoke.

'Get behind the trough, Red,' Palomino urged as he continued to fire the smoking rifle into the depths of the dust cloud. 'Take cover with Charlie.'

'Quit gabbing and start picking them varmints off, Kid,' Red said as he fired from the boardwalk.

Then the five riders emerged from the dust. Their mounts reared up in terror as their masters blasted more and more bullets at the lawmen.

One bullet ripped the hat from Red's head and he doubled in pain. He fell on to his knees and clutched his head and crawled back to the doorframe.

With the sound of firing still echoing in his ears, Red stared at the blood on his gloved hand. He rested on one knee and began reloading the smoking rifle.

'I've bin grazed, Kid,' Red shouted.

'It's a good job you ain't my height, Red.' Palomino leapt over the trough and crouched down at its side as he exchanged his empty Winchester for the one Charlie had just reloaded.

Charlie tugged on Palomino's sleeve. He drew the youngster's attention.

'I'm all out of bullets, boy,' the elderly lawman said. 'Make 'em count.'

'I'll try my best.' Palomino checked his own belt. He had only a few bullets remaining himself. He then inspected his handguns and shook his head. He hadn't reloaded the two matched Colts since last using them. He had only three fresh bullets in the weapon's dozen chambers. 'Reckon I'll have to stop missing, huh?'

'Good,' Charlie sighed rolling his eyes. 'At this rate we'll end up throwing rocks at them.'

Palomino cranked the hand guard. A spent casing flew from the rifle's magazine as the deputy raised the Winchester and eased its stock into the groove of his shoulder.

Carson's men suddenly transferred their lethal lead in Red's direction. Window panes shattered sending fragments of glass all over the boardwalk. Lumps of wood were torn from the side of the door frame forcing Red to press his backbone against the door.

'Keep drawing their fire, Red,' Palomino shouted as he levelled the rifle and rested its hot barrel on the rim of the trough. 'Keep drawing their fire.'

Within only a few heart-stopping moments the air was thick with acrid gunsmoke as Palomino tried to hit the horsemen who were shielded by the swirling mist. Shot after shot came at the Kid as he held his nerve and waited for a clear target.

Then he saw one of the Brand brothers emerge from the dense smoke. As Amos Brand sat on his nervous gelding and forced fresh bullets into the magazine of his carbine, Palomino squeezed gently on his trigger.

The rifle shuddered in his hands as a flash of flames and smoke erupted from the Winchester's barrel. As he rocked on his knees he knew that he had finally hit one of them.

Amos Brand lifted off his saddle and crashed heavily into the dry sand between the other horses. Palomino pushed the hand guard down and then dragged it back up. Another metal casing flew over his shoulder as the young deputy squinted through the heat haze and smoke at the lifeless body upon the sand.

'Good shot, Kid,' Red praised.

The lawman was about to smile when he heard the nerve-shattering noise only grief can muster. Palomino swallowed hard but his throat was dry. There was no spittle. He glanced down at Charlie.

'What in tarnation is that, Kid?' the old lawman asked.

'I ain't too sure,' Palomino answered.

Then another sound filled the street. It was pounding hoofs as a horse came thundering out of the mist and was being driven straight toward them.

Kid Palomino stared straight into the eyes of Luke Brand as he got closer and closer. The outlaw was fuelled by rage and grief unlike anything the deputy had ever witnessed before.

'Holy smoke,' Palomino gasped as he watched the rider lash his long leathers across the tail of his horse and charge away from Carson and his cronies toward the trough.

Red tried to fire his rifle but its red-hot mechanism jammed. The deputy screamed at Palomino.

'Kill him, Kid,' Red called out as another volley of bullets bore down on him.

Charlie poked Palomino in the ribs. 'You heard him, boy. Kill that varmint before he kills us.'

The unearthly sound of revenge had burned into Palomino's mind like a branding iron. He had never heard anything like it before. Brand's vocal curses echoed around the street. Desperately Palomino raised the rifle to his shoulder again but it was too late.

Luke Brand suddenly burst through the dust with his six-gun blazing. Obeying its rider's thrusting spurs, the horse jumped and cleared the water trough. The outstretched hoofs of the outlaw's mount hit the rifle clean out of Palomino's hands. The Kid ducked as the hefty horse and rider landed just beyond the startled deputy. Brand dragged his reins back and charged at Palomino. The startled lawman was knocked violently off his feet and careered headlong across the sand as the avenging outlaw fired down from his high perch.

Palomino came to an abrupt halt when he hit the edge of the boardwalk. He shook the dust from his face and rubbed the blood away from his grazed features. To his horror he watched as the horse cornered and blocked his escape as Brand straddled the gelding and reloaded his smoking six-shooter.

'You're gonna pay for killing my brother, boy,' Brand snarled at the dazed young Palomino. 'Pay with your life.'

Still unable to see anything but a colourful blur, the old lawman staggered up off the ground beside the trough and squinted hard at the snarling rider.

Charlie knew that the Kid was in trouble and needed help.

'Quit yelling like a dried-up old schoolmarm,' the veteran shouted as his hand found his holstered old six-shooter and pulled it clear. 'If'n you wanna shout at someone, shout at me.'

Luke Brand pushed the reloaded cylinder back into the heart of the smoking gun and secured it. His eyes glanced back at the intrepid old man as Charlie pulled on his trigger and unleashed a rod of deafening flame.

The bullet passed well over the horseman's head.

'That was your last mistake, old man.' Brand's thumb pulled back on his hammer and then aimed his .45 at Charlie. He fired and watched as the skinny remnant of a once sturdy lawman staggered and fell backward. A wave of water lashed over the sides of the trough as the old man sank into its shallow depths.

The water in the trough turned a sickening shade of scarlet. Only bubbles escaped the watery tomb.

It seemed like an eternity to the bruised and battered Palomino but it had been less than sixty seconds since Brand's horse had leapt over the trough and crashed into him. The dust still hung in the bright sunshine as it had not had time to settle.

Blood trickled from Palomino's mouth as it slowly

dawned on his dazed mind what had just happened. His attempts to get up off the sand were futile as Brand's horse crashed into his already bloodied body. No matter how desperately he attempted to get back on to his feet, the outlaw denied him. The sturdy quarter horse lowered its head and knocked Palomino off his feet again.

Palomino glanced at the trough. The old lawman was nowhere to be seen. Then he recalled the shot and sound of splashing and realized where his cantankerous pal was.

'Charlie,' the Kid called out. There was no reply.

With blood running from his nose and mouth, Palomino attempted to find his pair of match six-shooters. The horse was unwilling for its master's prey to succeed. The Kid raised his arms to shield himself from further injury as the powerful horse reared up and lashed out with its hoofs. Every instinct in Palomino's soul wanted to fight but he was reduced to merely defending his already battered body.

The young deputy was forced into a huddle as his hands searched for his guns. Then the snorting horse lowered its head and butted him. He coughed and spat blood at the sand as he tried to escape the continuous attack.

The sound of haunting laughter rained down on

him. He glanced up at the face of Luke Brand. The horseman was determined to make him pay for killing his brother and Palomino knew that his death would not be swift. Brand intended to draw every scrap of life from his victim before he finally killed him.

The Kid managed to force himself up to his feet but his victory was short-lived. Brand drove his spurs into the flanks of his horse and the animal charged into Palomino. The deputy crashed down against the rim of the boardwalk. He fell on to his face and gasped for air as the devilish Luke Brand levelled his weapon at him.

'You ready to die, star-packer?' Brand's words dragged the Kid back into consciousness. He stared up with glazed eyes at the horseman as Brand added, 'Are you busted up enough?'

'I've had worse,' Palomino lied as he felt the horse's breath on his grazed face. His mind raced to find a way to turn the tables on the outlaw. No matter how hard he searched for a solution, all he could do was stare into the gun barrel trained on him.

No cat had ever tormented a mouse quite as much as Brand mocked Palomino. All thoughts of avenging his brother had vanished from the outlaw's mind. Now Luke Brand was content to keep torturing his helpless victim to the very last drop of the deputy's blood.

'I've got me six bullets in this hog-leg, boy,' Brand snarled. 'I reckon I'll use every damn one of them before finishing you off.'

Kid Palomino had been in quite a few tough scrapes in his life but none of them like this. His eyes narrowed and stared up at the face of the horseman as he heard the hammer being locked into position once more.

'That's fine with me,' Palomino sighed heavily.

'Say your prayers, star-packer,' Brand growled as his finger curled around his trigger and aimed down at his trapped prey. 'This is for killing my brother Amos.'

Once again time appeared to have come to a standstill as the Kid stared up at the still-smoking gun barrel that was aimed at his head. His hand wiped the blood from his face and defiantly looked at the man who intended to be his executioner.

'Are you sure you don't wanna get a tad closer to me?' Kid Palomino forced a pained laugh. 'I'd hate for you to miss.'

Brand's expression changed as a storm fermented inside his ruthless guts. His hand was shaking with rage.

'I'll wipe that smile off your face with lead.'

'Shoot then,' Palomino spat. 'I ain't scared.'

A gruesome smile etched the outlaw's face as he leaned his bulk over the neck of his horse.

'Anything to oblige,' Brand hissed.

A thunderous shot echoed along the street.

EIGHT

The sound of a shot rang out in the street and echoed off the surrounding structures. Palomino had gritted his teeth as he awaited death, yet death did not visit the young deputy. The Grim Reaper had chosen another target for his inevitable wrath. The startled Kid watched as the outlaw arched on his saddle and gave a sickening grunt.

The gun curled on his finger and hung for a few moments as the sound of the solitary shot resonated in the Kid's ears. Then it fell from Brand's trigger finger and landed upon the churned-up sand as the brutalized horse backed away from Palomino.

Confusion filled the deputy's mind. He watched as the outlaw rocked on his saddle. Palomino steadied himself and stared at the outlaw. Brand's expression was one he had seen many times during his life as a lawman. It was the look only death can paint upon a face.

Hollow eyes looked down with unseeing bewilderment at the bullet hole in his chest. Blood squirted from the devilishly accurate wound in the middle of his chest as Brand slowly slid off his high-shouldered mount. The outlaw hit the ground yet one of his boots remained hooked in the stirrup. The skittish horse cantered down the street, dragging Brand beside it until the boot finally was pulled from the foot.

Palomino watched as Brand rolled like a rag doll on the sun-drenched sand before coming to a rest.

Red staggered through the gunsmoke and dropped down beside his young pal. He holstered his six-gun and then helped Palomino to his feet before glancing across at his handiwork.

'Don't look so damn surprised, Kid,' the older deputy said as he moved to the lifeless Brand and kicked sand in his face before returning to his pal. 'I told you that I could shoot.'

Palomino looked up at his friend.

'I sure wish you'd done that a whole lot earlier, Red,' the Kid sighed as he rubbed his aching ribs. 'I almost got kicked to death.'

Red raised his hands and shrugged. 'My damn rifle jammed, Kid. I tried to draw my gun but Carson and them two other varmints had me penned in.'

Palomino shielded his eyes against the sun and stared down the street. Only the body of Amos Brand remained beside his horse. Carson and his hired guns were gone.

'Carson high-tailed it?' he asked.

'Yep, they just whipped their horse's tails and rode on out of here a couple of minutes back,' Red replied as he looked all around them and then rubbed the nape of his neck. 'Where's Charlie?'

The Kid's eyes widened as horror etched his face.

'Hell!' Palomino swung on his boot leather and ran to the trough. He stared down into the murky water and felt panic overwhelm his bruised form. 'Help me get him out of here.'

Red rapidly moved to the opposite side of the trough and reached down into the water. They gripped the old man's arms and legs then fished him out.

Ignoring his own painful injuries, Palomino carefully scooped the bedraggled Charlie up in his arms and steadied himself. He forced himself away from the trough and started along the blisteringly hot street.

'I'm taking Charlie to the doc's,' the Kid gasped.

'What happened, Kid?' Red asked as Palomino staggered with the limp body in his arms. 'How'd

Charlie get in there?'

The young deputy continued walking as best he could. 'This brave old critter tried to draw that bastard's fire away from me, Red.'

'Holy cow.' Red trailed his friend toward the home of Fargo's only medical man. 'Charlie sure drew that varmint's fire OK. He looks dead to me.'

The younger deputy's eyes darted at his pal. There was a fire burning within them.

'Charlie ain't dead,' the Kid insisted before adding, 'not until the doc says he's dead anyway.'

Red did not dare utter another word. He knew that Palomino was right. Nobody was truly dead until the doc said so.

Kid Palomino kept walking even though every sinew in his bruised and bleeding frame told him that it was useless. He knew that if Charlie had not drawn Brand's attention away from himself for those precious few seconds, the outlaw would have simply shot him as he had intended.

As they reached the small house at the end of Fargo's main thoroughfare Palomino sucked in air, stepped up on to the rickety boardwalk and kicked the small gate off its hinges.

The shooting had awoken most of the town's citizens but Doc Black's front door was still shut. The Kid paused and was about to kick it out of its frame when it swung open and the elderly medic ushered him into the building.

Red rested his wrists on the picket fence and stared silently into the darkened interior of the wooden structure. After what felt like a lifetime, the Kid wandered back out into the sunshine.

Red rubbed his unshaven jaw and watched as Palomino brushed past him and sat down on the edge of the walkway. The young deputy looked down at the sand at his feet but said nothing.

It was obvious to Red that he had been correct about Charlie, but not to his young pal. Palomino had to have time to let the truth sink in. The older deputy was about to speak when the sound of movement behind his broad shoulders drew his attention back to the small house. Red turned and stared at the old medical man as he approached the open door and looked straight at him.

The grim face of the doc answered the question that was burning in his craw. Doc Black shook his head and then sorrowfully closed his door.

'Charlie's gone, Kid,' Red sighed heavily.

Seated on the dusty boards, Palomino nodded in acceptance of the gruesome fact. He then got back to his feet and exhaled loudly.

'C'mon, Red.'

'Where we going?'

Palomino paused and looked straight at his friend's face.

'We're going to get our horses,' he snorted. 'We got some outlaws to round up. We got a score to settle.'

Even though Red knew that they should wait for Sheriff Lomax to return to Fargo, he also knew by experience that it was never wise to argue with Kid Palomino.

Not when he was hurting and the Kid was hurting real bad.

As they made their way back to their awaiting horses outside the sheriff's office, Palomino stopped and stared to where they had first set eyes on Bill Carson and his hirelings.

'I reckon we'd best go check on Stan Hardwick, Red,' the Kid said. 'Him and his ladies might need our help.'

Neither Palomino nor Red could imagine the horror they were about to find as they casually strode up to the elegant house and entered.

Their gruesome discovery only a few moments later within the confines of the banker's home would spur both battle-weary lawmen to avenge the shocking outrage. They retraced their steps and paused in the rear yard for a few moments. They looked as though every drop of colour had been drained from their faces.

The Kid glanced at Red. 'Let's get back to the office and get our horses ready.'

The older man nodded. 'I'll call in the funeral parlour on the way, Kid. He can sort this mess out.'

Palomino tightened his gloves.

'I'll leave a note pinned to the billboard for the sheriff,' he drawled angrily as he vainly tried to dismiss the sight that was branded into his mind. 'I'll tell him where we're headed and ask him to rustle up a posse to follow.'

Red nodded and thought about the brutal slayings they had just discovered. 'How can anyone do something like that, Kid?'

'I don't know,' Palomino answered. 'But I swear by all that's holy, Carson and his boys will never do nothing like this again, Red.'

Both lawman headed back into the heart of Fargo.

NINE

The sight that had greeted the deputies had chilled them to the bone. Neither lawman had ever seen anything like the savagery they had discovered in the home of the banker. It was clear to Palomino that the notorious Bill Carson was probably far worse than even the law realized. The Kid wondered how many other times had Carson simply dispatched all the witnesses to his lurid crimes in a similar fashion, so that they could never be linked to him.

Palomino hooked his stirrup over the horn of his saddle and tightened the cinch strap as his fellow deputy came out of the office with two fully loaded Winchesters and a box of cartridges. He stepped down into the sunshine and slid one of the rifles into the mount's saddle scabbard. He lifted the leather flap of his saddle-bags and pushed the ammunition into the satchel.

The Kid lowered his fender and caught the repeating rifle his pal threw to him. He pushed the gleaming barrel into his own scabbard and then looked over his high-shouldered stallion.

'Are we ready?' he asked Rivers as he pulled his long leathers free of the hitching pole.

'We got us a few extra canteens of water and some vittles,' Red replied as he patted his quarter horse and ducked under its reins. 'We got rifles and enough bullets to fend off the 7th cavalry.'

'That should do.' Kid backed the palomino stallion away from the office and then grabbed the horse's cream-coloured mane and stepped into the stirrup. He mounted in one fluid action and then gathered up his loose reins and watched as his friend duplicated his actions.

Palomino leaned on to his saddle horn and stared at the now busy street that faced them. He tilted his head and looked at his partner.

'Which way did them bastards head, Red?' he asked.

Red pointed. 'They was headed for the desert, Kid.'

Palomino grimaced and then sighed, 'The desert is gonna be mighty hot at this time of day but I reckon I know it a whole lot better than they do.'

'It ain't even noon yet, boy,' Red remarked. 'That desert is gonna get hotter than hell before it starts to calm down again.'

The Kid patted the neck of his handsome horse and shrugged as he steadied the powerful animal beneath his saddle.

'As long as we've got enough water for these horses I ain't worried, Red,' he stated firmly.

'You figure we can catch up with them *hombres*?' Red asked as he swung the quarter horse around and trotted to the side of his friend. 'They've got a mighty good start on us, Kid.'

Palomino nodded. 'Yep. We'll catch up with them though.'

Both horsemen glanced around the wooden structures and the tall red brick bank before steadying themselves on their hot saddles. It was something they always did without even knowing that they were doing it. It was as though they were taking a last look at the settlement in case they never returned from their often perilous missions.

'Nugget's ready,' Palomino told his pal.

Red leaned over the neck of his mount. 'Are you ready, Derby?'

The quarter horse shook its head. Both men raised their eyebrows and gave out a mutual yell. The horses thundered through the shimmering heat haze in the direction that Red had pointed to a few moments before.

The determined duo stood in their stirrups and thundered between the countless people who now filled the street as the sun slowly rose in the cloudless blue heavens.

It would get hotter, just like they figured. Hotter than hell in more ways than anyone might imagine before the day was through.

TEN

The rattling chains of the stagecoach echoed off the scattering of buildings, which were known collectively as Dry Gulch. Those who were not sleeping during the unrelenting sunshine sat on weathered hardback chairs and pondered the shadows that slowly indicated the passing of time. Dry Gulch was a place that only survived at the edge of the desert because of its deep wells and crystal clear water. Yet the overwhelming heat had always kept the population to a bare minimum.

Shaded by porch overhangs the onlookers puffed on pipes and watched as the Overland Stage came to an abrupt halt outside the solitary saloon. The Busted Wheel was by far the largest building within the confines of Dry Gulch. It oozed a powerful aroma of stale perfume, spilled liquor and tobacco smoke.

The driver beat the dust off his clothing and wrapped his reins around the brakepole. He leaned over, looked down at the side of the coach and bellowed.

'Dry Gulch.'

The carriage door opened and the well-dressed Deacon disembarked with elegant ease. He held his ivory-topped cane under his arm as the driver handed down his canvas bag.

'Thank you, driver,' he said touching the brim of his hat and turning to face the large saloon. 'Do they have rooms to rent here?'

'Yep, and they also got females to rent as well,' the driver chuckled and then carefully descended to the boardwalk and pushed his way past the man who looked like a gambler in his rush to quench his thirst.

Danby Deacon smiled to himself and then followed the bearded stagecoach driver into the saloon. The smell greeted him before his eyes adjusted to the far dimmer interior. It was in total contrast to the blazing sun of the street. The driver had already finished his first whiskey before Deacon had walked across the sawdust-covered floor.

The bartender looked long and hard at the

elegant Deacon as he slowly walked with bag in one hand and the other swinging his cane to match his stride.

'What in hell is that?' the bartender asked the driver as he poured the thirsty man another full glass of whiskey.

The driver glanced over his shoulder at Deacon and then returned his attention to the glass in his hand.

'A gambler,' he sniffed as he filled his mouth with the fiery liquor and swallowed. 'Picked him up in Cherokee Springs. Why in hell anyone would wanna come here beats me.'

The scrawny bartender shook his head as he polished a glass with his apron bib.

'He sure looks awful neat, even for a gambler,' he remarked. 'I ain't ever seen a gambler look quite so neat before. It just ain't natural.'

'And he's a lousy poker player, Hyram,' the driver noted. 'I sure don't know where he gets his money from 'coz it ain't from being able to play cards.'

A wry smile came to the bartender's face. 'That's mighty interesting. I might challenge the dude to a few games of stud.'

'He dresses up a storm though.' The driver sighed. 'He's got himself a gold stick pin holding down his bib.'

Danby Deacon reached the bar counter, glanced at the stagecoach driver and smiled.

'Cravat, my good man. It's called a cravat,' Deacon corrected and patted the dusty driver on the back. He coughed as a cloud of trail dust wafted over the counter and then placed a fifty dollar gold piece down on its wooden surface. 'A bottle of your best sipping whiskey and a box of your finest cigars. If this establishment has such items.'

'We got 'em, mister,' the bartender said.

The driver looked at Deacon. 'That's a lot of whiskey for one man to guzzle on his lonesome.'

Deacon nodded in agreement. 'Two bottles of whiskey, barkeep. One for my friend here.'

The stagecoach driver beamed. 'Well thank you kindly.'

'My pleasure.' Deacon looked at the bartender as the man placed two bottles of amber liquor down on the wet surface and then plucked a box of cigars from a shelf at his side. 'Anything else, mister?'

Deacon smiled and glanced around the tobacco-stained interior of the Busted Wheel. 'Where are the whores?'

Both men chuckled.

'They'll be here soon enough, dude.' The driver winked as he picked up one of the bottles and tucked it under his coat and turned on his heels.

Deacon watched the driver sway as he walked back toward the bright street. 'You'll smell them before you see them.'

Danby Deacon turned to the man who was still polishing glasses on the other side of the counter.

'Where's he going?' he asked the bartender.

'He's got to drive the stage to Poison Flats.'

Deacon rubbed his jaw. 'He's going to drive a six-horse team in that condition?'

'Hell, he can drive even when he's sober,' the lean bartender replied before testing the gold coin with his teeth and then pocketing it.

Deacon raised his eyebrows. 'Keep the change.'

'I already have.'

ELEVEN

The tracks left by the Carson gang's horses' hoofs were easily followed in and around Fargo but the further north they ventured toward the arid desert, the harder it was for the intrepid pair of deputies to follow. Every mark left in the white sand soon disappeared. It was so fine and dry its granules filled in every impression a few seconds after it was made.

Yet somehow young Kid Palomino seemed to instinctively know where the three riders were headed. He kept encouraging the tall golden stallion beneath his saddle on, to the bewilderment of his pal.

'Admit it, Kid,' Red said nervously as he trailed his determined friend deeper into the unfamiliar terrain. 'Them *hombres* could have headed anywhere. We ain't got a chance of catching them.'

Palomino had been strangely quiet since they had discovered the bodies of Hardwick and the three females. The young deputy had a gritty determination festering in him that refused to even consider defeat. He glanced back at his pal and slowed his mount so the smaller horse could draw level with him.

'Stop fretting, Red,' he snapped. 'I know exactly where Carson and his men are headed. I figured it out before we even left Fargo.'

Red mopped the sweat from his face with the tails of his bandanna and exhaled loudly. 'I ain't calling you a liar, boy, but you ain't yourself. You're dripping with revenge and its messing with your head. Nobody could find them in this inferno. It just ain't possible.'

Palomino grinned. 'Nothing's impossible, Red.'

Red shook his head as the horses headed up a slight rise of soft sand. Both men had to stand in their stirrups and urge the lathered-up mounts up the slope. With every step an avalanche of loose sand rolled down the ridge they were climbing.

As the exhausted horses reached the flat top of the ridge they eased back on their reins and stopped the animals. The top of a dune offered them a panoramic view of the arid terrain they had doggedly ridden into. Yet wherever they cast their attention all they could see was a desolate ocean of golden sand. The distance was blurred by a curtain of boiling air that rippled and played tricks with their tired eyes, yet Palomino was still confident that he knew exactly where their prey had headed.

Red Rivers did not share his partner's enthusiasm. He was scared and it showed. The veteran lawman had faced many heavily armed outlaws in his career but the blistering sun and the arid landscape frightened him.

'We'd best turn back, Palomino,' Red sighed as he checked his canteens nervously. 'They ain't nowhere to be seen and we're running low on water.'

'Easy, Red,' the Kid said as he removed his hat briefly to wipe the sweat off his brow. 'I know where they've gone.'

A tormented expression filled Red's features. 'How can you tell which way they've gone? There ain't nothing out there but sand and nowhere to take cover from the sun. I'm as riled up as you are but I ain't hankering to commit suicide trying to catch them throat-cutting bastards. We just gotta head back to Fargo while there's still time.'

The Kid dismounted and dropped his hat on to the ground and then poured a good ration of water into the upturned bowl for his mount to drink. He stared at his friend who carefully slid from his saddle and watered his own mount.

'This is loco, Kid,' Red muttered as the horses drank their meagre ration of water. 'You're gonna get us killed on a hunch.'

With wisdom far beyond his years, Palomino scooped up his hat and returned it to his head and shrugged. The droplets of water trapped within the bowl felt good as they cooled him.

'I know exactly where they've gone,' Palomino said bluntly and then poked his boot in his stirrup and dragged himself back on to his saddle. He waited for his partner to do the same and then tapped his spurs against the creamy flanks of his mount. 'You coming or are you gonna turn-tail and ride back?'

Red thought for a moment and then urged his quarter horse to follow the majestic stallion of his friend. 'Hold up, Kid. I ain't finished gabbing yet.'

The younger deputy glanced at his partner. 'I've finished listening to you moaning and groaning, Red. I tell you I've figured out where they're headed and I'm headed there too.'

Red Rivers lifted his wet pants off the sweat-filled saddle and glanced at Palomino as they continued to allow their mounts to walk between two steep dunes. No matter how hard he racked his brain, he could not figure out how Palomino could possibly tell where the outlaws could have ridden in this terrain.

'How can you know where Carson and his galoots have gone, Kid?' he asked before sitting back down. 'Tell me, how can you be certain where they're headed?'

'You'll figure it out just like I did,' Palomino said as his unblinking eyes stared into the shimmering heat vapour before them.

'My brain's boiling inside my head, Kid,' Red grunted. 'My figuring ain't so good in this temperature.'

They steered their trusty mounts down through a narrow canyon of bleached rocks. The heat grew more intense as they travelled the winding course. Both men could feel the merciless rays of the overhead sun bearing down on them as they rode side by side into the sickening abyss.

Yet Palomino continued to lead them as though he had travelled this route many times before. Red could not fathom how the younger horseman was able to negotiate this unfamiliar place. Had Palomino noticed something that his partner had failed to observe? Thoughtfully, Red chewed on the tails of his bandanna and watched as the Kid defiantly continued to lead the way.

The shimmering heat haze bent the air before them. Nothing was exactly as they imagined it to be.

It was as though they were looking into a powerful waterfall and not blisteringly hot air.

Suddenly as the horses turned a rugged corner of bleached rock, they both saw the very thing that the Kid had spotted two hours earlier.

A line of poles stretched from one horizon to the other held together by telegraph wires marked a dusty road. The wires glistened in the unforgiving sun as they swayed back and forth between the weathered poles. The dusty road was between the riders and the poles.

Palomino drew rein first and leaned back against his cantle. Red slowly halted his mount and stared at the poles in bewildered awe.

'If that don't beat all,' Red sighed.

'That's how I know which way they went, Red.' The Kid picked up one of his canteens and took a welcome swig of its warm contents.

Red turned his head. 'Telegraph poles?'

'Exactly,' Palomino confirmed. 'Telegraph poles.'

'How the hell do they tell you where Bill Carson and his gang have gone, Kid?' Red growled. 'Go on, tell me how them poles can possibly tell you where them bastards have gone.'

Palomino smiled and handed his canteen across the distance between them. The older horseman grabbed the canteen and took a long swallow of the precious liquid.

'Feel better?' the Kid asked as he accepted the canteen and returned its stopper to the leather vessel's neck.

Red sighed heavily. 'I'm obliged for the drink, Kid, but this is driving me plumb loco. I just don't understand what you're getting at.'

'To my knowledge, Carson and his cronies ain't ever bin in this territory before, Red,' Palomino explained as he hung the canteen beside the others next to his cutting rope. 'This is mighty dangerous country and not to be taken lightly. Think about it, Carson and his men knew who owned the bank back in Fargo and they knew where Hardwick and his family lived. They must have bin given this information by someone else.'

Red screwed up his eyes. 'I'm with you so far.'

'It wasn't an accident that Carson rode in here and knew where Hardwick lived. That gang rode into Fargo and followed detailed instructions so that they wouldn't run into any trouble robbing the bank,' the Kid continued to explain. 'They would have gotten away with it if they hadn't have run into us when they were making their escape. It stands to reason that they were also instructed on how to get out of this territory.'

Red stared blankly at his pal. 'But what have these

telegraph poles got to do with you being able to figure out where them *hombres* are headed, Kid?'

Palomino indicated to the poles. 'The telegraph wires head on out of Fargo, don't they? Then they split into two sections. One section heads east and the other heads west.'

Red Rivers pulled out his tobacco pouch and started to roll a cigarette. 'I know that. So what?'

'The wires head east to Cherokee Springs and west to Dry Gulch.' Palomino watched as Red struck a match and lit his cigarette. 'Cherokee Springs is too far away from Fargo to ride to with saddle-bags full of money, Red. You'd have to travel there by stagecoach but Dry Gulch is only just over that rise.'

Red stared through his cigarette smoke. 'It is?'

Palomino nodded. 'It surely is. I reckon it's only a few miles away from here.'

The wily deputy looked long and hard at Palomino.

'How'd you know that, Kid?' Red sat up on his saddle and frowned. 'I know for a fact that you ain't ever ridden out this way before. How'd you know that Dry Gulch is only a couple of miles away?'

Kid Palomino shook his head in frustration and checked his pair of matched Colts. Then he glanced at his bewildered pal.

'Ain't you ever looked at the big map on the wall

in the telegraph office back in Fargo, Red?' Palomino gathered up his reins again and looked at the daunting terrain still ahead of them. 'That map has got all the poles marked on it. That's in case they gotta send out linemen to fix them.'

'They got a map in the telegraph office?' Red asked as he sucked the smoke through the cigarette and then blew it at the cloudless sky.

'A real big map for all to see,' the Kid nodded and then guided the high-shouldered palomino stallion to the rough road of compacted sand.

Red tossed the cigarette away, tapped his spurs and navigated the distance to the dusty trail. He looked down at the road and observed the wheel grooves cut into the ground.

'You can see the ruts where the stagecoach travels up and down this road, Kid,' he said before noticing that his partner was staring down at something else marked in the sand.

Palomino eased his tall stallion beside his pal's horse and studied the sand carefully. He raised a hand and pointed down at fresh hoof tracks.

'There,' he muttered before dismounting and kneeling beside the tracks. He could not contain the sense of gratification he felt in finding the fresh tracks.

Red leaned over the neck of his mount. 'What you

doing, Palomino boy?'

The Kid straightened up and then grabbed the mane of his mount. He threw himself back up on to his saddle and mopped his brow with his shirt sleeve.

'Fresh hoof tracks,' he pointed out.

'That's the stagecoach horse's tracks, Kid,' Red sighed.

'No they ain't. These tracks weren't left by the stage team.'

Palomino pointed at the deep hoof marks six feet away from the wheel rim grooves. 'They're the hoof tracks of three horses that were headed west.'

'To Dry Gulch?'

Palomino grinned. 'Yep, to Dry Gulch.'

'Why'd you figure they're headed there for, Palomino?' Red wondered.

The younger deputy glanced at his pal. 'I bet it's to meet up with the *hombre* who planned the bank robbery and split their ill-gotten gains, Red.'

'The what?' Red raised his bushy eyebrows.

'The loot, Red,' Palomino said slowly. 'They've gone to Dry Gulch to split the loot.'

Finally it dawned on the older lawman what his partner was talking about. 'Now I get it.'

Kid Palomino rolled his eyes. 'I'm sure happy that you now understand what I've bin talking about for the last few hours.'

'Next time talk clearer, Kid,' Red scolded. 'How's a body meant to know what you mean when you keep gabbing about telegraph poles?'

The Kid silently frowned.

Then without warning Red suddenly slapped the sides of his quarter horse with his boot leather and galloped away from Palomino. The older lawman glanced over his shoulder and shouted, 'What you waiting for? C'mon, Kid. Let's go get 'em.'

Kid Palomino steadied the handsome stallion. 'Catch that old rooster, Nugget.'

The powerful horse bolted into action and chased the quarter horse. The Kid rose off his saddle, balanced in his stirrups and cracked the tails of his long leathers in the desert air.

Within a few heartbeats the stallion had caught up to the far smaller horse. As Palomino drew level he looked at his old pal and winked. Red Rivers touched his hat brim and nodded as their horses defied their exhaustion and kept thundering on to Dry Gulch.

Neither of the deputies had any idea of what lay ahead of them in the aptly named Dry Gulch. All they knew for certain was that they were closing in on the merciless outlaws. Men of Bill Carson's formidable reputation were all cut from the same cloth.

They would fight to their last drop of blood and

take as many innocent folks with them as they could before they succumbed. Their evil breed did not die easy.

Soon there would be a clash of titanic proportions within the arid town the deputies were quickly approaching, for neither Kid Palomino nor his sidekick Red Rivers had ever shied away from a fight when they knew that right was on their side.

The lawmen rode on.

TWELVE

A growing worry was gnawing at the mature outlaw's innards as his eyes kept glancing at the wall clock hanging from a rusty nail in the small office. He knew that time was quickly passing and wondered how much of it was left before the law finally showed up in the remote town.

Bill Carson was sat opposite Jeff Kane and Poke Peters inside the Dry Gulch telegraph office waiting for the pre-arranged message from the Deacon. Yet as the clock ticked loudly there had not been any indication that the message was going to arrive.

The gang had been there for over an hour and were getting more and more anxious. The grim-faced Carson rose from the hardback chair, strode to the wooden counter and glared over it at the small figure sat beside the telegraph key pad.

A fury was brewing inside the notorious killer as he clenched both his fists and watched the weedy man, who only seemed to awaken when a message caused the crude machinery to start tapping like a frantic woodpecker.

Poke Peters stood and moved to the side of Carson. He rubbed his throat and shook his head before turning to the stony-faced Carson.

'I thought you said that the Deacon would send us a message, Bill,' he asked the statuesque outlaw before glancing back at the still seated Kane. 'Me and Jeff figured he was totally professional but this don't sit right in my guts. What are we meant to do?'

Beneath the wide brim of his Stetson, Carson's eyes darted at Peters. 'Something feels mighty wrong to me about this, Poke. You're right.'

Peters nodded in agreement.

'I don't like this hanging around,' he said. 'We should have left this cesspit by now. Every damn minute we wait in here, the closer the law is getting, Bill.'

'Yeah.' Carson knew that Peters was correct.

They were wasting time and time was the one thing they were mighty low on.

Kane got to his feet and strode to where his fellow outlaws stood. He tilted his head and stared between the pair at the sleeping telegraph operator.

'Them telegraph keys ain't made a sound since we arrived here, Bill,' he commented before resting his hands on his holstered guns hidden beneath his long dust coat. 'Maybe it's busted.'

Carson and Peters looked at Kane.

'How would you know if it's busted?' Peters asked.

The older and far more dangerous of the men stroked his unshaven jaw and narrowed his icy glare. 'You could be right. For all we know there might be a break in the wires. The Deacon might have sent me his instructions but his instructions ain't reached here.'

Kane and Peters looked troubled by the prospect.

'What'll we do, Bill?' Kane wondered. 'We can't hang around here waiting for a message that might not even arrive.'

Peters leaned closer to his fellow outlaws and drawled in a low whisper. 'I got me a feeling in my craw that them star-packers back at Fargo will be rounding up a posse when they find the banker and them women.'

Bill Carson nodded in agreement. 'Yeah, you're right.'

Peters glanced briefly at the dozing operator and then returned his attention to Carson.

'What do you figure we should do, Bill?' he asked

nervously before pacing to the office windows and looking out into the sunlit street. 'We've already wasted over an hour in this damn town and if they do send out a posse from Fargo we're in real big trouble.'

'They could arrive here at any time,' Kane swallowed hard.

'I ain't scared of any posse,' Carson snapped viciously at his hired guns. 'But you're right. We have wasted a big chunk of time here and no mistake. If there is a posse looking for us they'll be getting mighty close.'

Kane looked at Carson. 'Let's high-tail it, Bill.'

'Jeff's right,' Peters nodded. 'I reckon we should split the takings and ride. It ain't our fault the Deacon hasn't sent you a message, Bill.'

'It ain't his neck them star-packers will be itching to stretch,' Kane added. 'We gotta get out of here.'

The grim-faced Carson stared at the sleeping old man beyond the counter. 'The Deacon said that we should sell our horses and take the stagecoach to Yuma like ordinary folks. Trouble is there ain't no stagecoach.'

'I ain't selling my horse,' Kane announced.

'Me neither.' Peters spat at the floor.

The fearsome Carson rubbed his jaw and looked at the telegraph operator as he slumbered on a note pad. The outlaw slammed his fist down on the wooden counter. The noise shook the building and caused the small man to wake. His bleary eyes squinted through his spectacles at the three awesome creatures facing him.

'Are you boys still here?' he yawned.

Carson pointed a gloved finger at the bony old character.

'Check that your telegraph is working, old timer,' he ordered.

The telegraph operator raised his eyebrows. 'What on earth for? It's working just fine.'

Furiously, Carson lifted the wooden flap and walked toward the still sleepy old man. As he reached the desk he drew one of his six-shooters and cocked its hammer. He pushed the cold steel barrel under the nose of the seated man.

'Humour me and do what I tell you,' the outlaw growled. 'Test that the lines are OK. I'll blow your head off your damn neck if you don't. Savvy?'

The old man gulped. 'I savvy.'

Carson watched and listened as the operator tapped on the keys. Within a few seconds the office resounded with the distinctive noise of the keys replying. The outlaw rose to his full height and holstered his gun.

'It's working just like this old fossil said it was,

boys,' Carson muttered at his men. He then glanced down at the terrified figure with his fingers poised in mid-air. 'When's the next stagecoach to Yuma due?'

The old man was still shaking as he gathered his thoughts.

'There's one due through here at sundown, sir,' he croaked. 'Yes, that's right. Sundown.'

Carson marched back to his men. 'We're going to the saloon and have us a drink. I gotta think.'

The telegraph operator watched as Carson grabbed the door handle and pulled the door toward him. Kane and Peters stepped out on to the boardwalk as Carson paused and glanced back at the frightened old man.

'If you get a message for Bill Carson, bring it straight to me at the saloon,' he demanded.

The fragile old timer nodded. 'I'll bring it to you as soon as it arrives.'

As the door slammed shut the operator opened a draw and pulled out a quart of whiskey and pulled its cork. He guzzled half its contents and then shook his head. There was something about looking into the eyes of the merciless Carson, which few men had ever done and lived to tell the tale.

The elderly telegraph operator downed the remaining half bottle of fiery amber liquor and glanced at the empty vessel in his hand.

'I sure hope it's good news that he's expecting,' he stammered in terror. 'I don't hanker giving him anything that might upset that varmint.'

THIRTEEN

The Broken Wheel saloon was like numerous others in the more desolate portions of the west. It towered over the other sun-washed structures so that anyone with a hankering to quench their thirst, lose their wages or get their itch scratched knew exactly where to go.

Bill Carson and his two dusty cohorts marched purposely across the parched sand toward the welcoming building. Carson stretched his long legs and stepped up on to the building's boardwalk. He paused for a few moments under the shade of the porch overhang as his fellow outlaws caught up with him. As Kane and Peters stepped up on to the boards, Carson ran a match down the wooden upright and cupped its flame as he lit the cigar between his teeth.

Like a sidewinder studying its next victim, his eyes darted around the virtually deserted street. He filled his lungs with the strong smoke and then shook the match before flicking its blackened remnants away.

Kane was edgy. Sweat dripped from his chin as he watched the deadly Carson staring at the saloon's hitching rail where they had tethered their mounts upon entering Dry Gulch and heading for the telegraph office. Kane had made no secret of the fact that he wanted to be paid his share of the proceeds and ride. Carson looked at the hefty bags secured to his mount and then looked at Kane.

'You get them bags and tote them into the saloon,' Carson ordered and then pointed a gloved finger at Peters. 'And you help him, Poke.'

There was no argument from either Peters or Kane. They stepped down into the blazing sun and started to undo the leather laces that kept the saddle-bags in place.

As his men did what he had told them to do, Carson placed a hand on the swing doors of the Busted Wheel and entered. The saloon was a lot cooler than the street but the outlaw did not appear to notice.

The half dozen souls within the weathered structure glanced at the tall figure as he strode across the sawdust-covered floor toward the bar counter.

Hyram Smith had been a bartender for years and always recognized trouble when it raised its ugly head. He picked up a glass and started to feverishly polish it with his apron as Carson slowly approached. With every step that the outlaw took, the bartender's heart pounded inside his chest. It was facing the Grim Reaper to watch Carson approach.

'Howdy stranger,' the terrified barkeep managed to say.

Carson did not utter a word as he walked toward the bar counter. He placed his boot on the brass rail and then rested one hand on the damp surface of the counter as he plucked his cigar from his lips.

'Whiskey,' he drawled through a cloud of smoke. 'A bottle of your best with an unbroken seal.'

The bartender nervously nodded and swiftly lifted a bottle off the shelf behind his narrow shoulders and placed it down before the rugged Carson.

'Is this brand to your liking?' the nervous bartender asked, as he carefully took a thimble glass from a pyramid of identical vessels and set it beside the bottle. 'This is the best in the house.'

Carson studied the label and then looked up.

'It'll do for now.'

Hyram Smith relaxed and continued to polish

glasses as the swing doors were flung apart again. He stared at Kane and Peters as they entered toting the saddle-bags. The bartender felt his throat tighten again as he watched them.

'Those bags sure look heavy,' he commented innocently.

A mere heartbeat later, Carson drew and pushed the barrel of his six-shooter under the chin of the bartender. Their eyes met as the leader of the greatly diminished band of outlaws stated to shake his head.

'You ain't seen no saddle-bags,' Carson growled before turning to face the rest of the seated saloon customers. 'None of you have seen no saddle-bags. Savvy?'

Every man within the Busted Wheel nodded in agreement. Carson returned his attention to Smith and started to stroke the seven-inch steel barrel across the feeble man's face.

'You ain't seen anything, have you?' Carson repeated before adding, 'You ain't seen no swollen saddle-bags and you ain't seen us. Remember that and you'll live a whole lot longer but if you start recalling this, you'll surely die.'

'I ain't seen nothing,' Smith stammered.

Carson smiled and holstered his gun. He glanced at Kane and Peters as they reached a table and placed the bags on its green baize surface.

'Howdy, gents,' the bartender greeted them.

The attention of Carson went from the bartender to his men as they rubbed the sweat from their grimy faces and strolled to the bar counter.

Suddenly the sound of giggling females above them on the landing attracted all their attention. The outlaws stared in amused disbelief at the sight of the elegantly attired man with his arms draped around the bargirl's shoulders.

'What in tarnation is that?' Kane grinned in amusement by the sight above them.

'Whatever it is, it's sure fancy,' Peters chuckled.

'It's just a gambler,' Carson dismissed the sight and broke the paper seal of the whiskey bottle. 'Don't pay him any heed, boys.'

Danby Deacon stepped to the top of the staircase and cleared his throat. Every eye in the saloon glanced at the man who seemed to want the attention of the three outlaws.

'What about me?' he called out. The two powdered females continued to giggle as Deacon lowered his arms and adjusted his cuffs as he smiled down at Carson and his men. 'I've seen the three of you desperados and those well-stuffed saddle-bags.'

'You'd best forget or you'll die, dude.' Carson sucked on his cigar and stared at the unusual sight of the man he had never before met. When his lungs were full of smoke he removed the cigar and dropped it into a spittoon at his feet. A loud hiss echoed inside the brass vessel as Carson pushed his coat tails over his holstered weaponry.

'Is that right, Bill?' Deacon started to walk slowly down the steps toward the older of the outlaws. He kept on smiling as he tapped his cane on the boards. 'You'd kill me just for having a good memory?'

Carson glanced to either side at his equally dumbfounded men as the immaculate Deacon continued to descend the staircase toward the bar.

'He called you by name, Bill,' Kane said.

'How does that dude know you?' Peters wondered.

Carson raised his thumb and scratched his chin. 'I don't know how that fancy hombre knows my name.'

Deacon laughed, 'We're old pals, boys.'

'Pals?' Carson repeated the word. 'I ain't ever set eyes on you before. How could we be pals?'

Deacon could see the hands of the notorious outlaw start to twitch as they hovered above his holstered guns. He kept smiling though.

'We've known each other for years,' the man who resembled a riverboat gambler announced. 'Haven't we, Bill?'

Peters and Kane could not believe their eyes or

their ears. They had never seen anybody face up to Carson before and it confused the pair.

There was something about Deacon that made Carson focus hard on him. It was as if they already knew one another and yet the outlaw could not recall ever meeting this flamboyant figure before. Deacon was not the sort of man anyone ever forgot once they had encountered him.

Carson gritted his teeth and squared up to the dandy who seemed totally unaware how dangerous it was to argue with obviously hardened outlaws.

'You know who I am, dude?' Carson raged.

Deacon paused as he reached the bottom of the steps and looked at his questioner. 'I certainly do. You're the infamous Bill Carson if I'm not mistaken, and I seldom am mistaken.'

Kane and Peters watched open-mouthed as Deacon defiantly strolled to the card table and then seated himself. He pulled out a silver case and opened its spring lid. He withdrew a cigar, bit off its tip and spat at the sawdust.

'Sit down, Bill,' Deacon said waving at the empty chairs and looking at the bags on the table before him. 'We've business to discuss.'

Carson glanced at his two cohorts and then dragged out a chair and sat down next to the fearless stranger.

'Who the hell are you?' Carson snarled like a rabid wolf at the smiling man as he watched the cigar being lit. 'How'd you know my name? You wouldn't happen to be a bounty hunter, would you?'

Both Kane and Peters chuckled at the suggestion.

Deacon blew the flame out and tossed the match at the sawdust floor. He inhaled deeply.

'I'm no bounty hunter, Bill,' he said wryly. 'But I know you. We've worked together for quite a while.'

The face of Bill Carson went blank as it slowly dawned on him who this man was. He dragged his chair closer to Deacon and studied him carefully.

'You can't be who I think you are,' he said.

Deacon raised an eyebrow, looked at the devilish outlaw and blew smoke at the saddle-bags. 'I was meant to wire you but I had a little trouble back at Cherokee Springs. So I caught a stage and came here personally.'

Carson looked at the saddle-bags and then at Deacon.

'Can you prove that you're him?' he asked.

'Oh, I'm the Deacon OK, Bill.'

The statement was like a lightning bolt and caused Carson to sit back on his chair and stare in disbelief at the man before him. Deacon looked more like a harmless riverboat gambler than the man who had planned the outlaw's most daring of robberies.

'Hell,' Carson cursed. 'You are the Deacon.'

Deacon raised his hand and indicated to the bartender. 'Bring that bottle and four glasses over here, friend.'

Hyram Smith did as instructed.

The females cooed like doves up on the landing and waved down at Deacon. He smiled at them and watched as Smith placed the whiskey bottle and glasses down between Carson and himself.

'Did it all go as I planned it, Bill?' he asked as he pulled the cork from the bottle neck and filled the four glasses.

Peters and Kane sat opposite the two men who were staring at one another intently. They accepted the two glasses of whiskey and made short work of them.

Carson frowned. 'Things went sour, Deacon.'

For the first time since Deacon had made his unexpected appearance the smile faded from his face. The glass of whiskey was close to his lips but after Carson had spoken he placed the glass down and tapped cigar ash on to the floor.

'What do you mean by that, Bill?' he pressed. 'My plans are always foolproof. How did they go sour?'

The rugged Carson rubbed his jaw and then downed his whiskey in one swift throw. He rubbed his face and then refilled his glass.

'Everything went exactly like you said it would, Deacon,' he started. 'Up until me and the boys left the banker's house and started heading out of town.'

Danby Deacon leaned forward. 'What happened as you were leaving Fargo, Bill? What?'

Carson exhaled and shook his head. 'Star-packers. We run into three star-packers.'

Danby Deacon stared in disbelief at Carson.

'That can't be.' Deacon raised his eyebrows and sucked hard on his cigar. 'The sheriff and his deputies were meant to be out of town. The only lawman in Fargo was that blind old coot who stands in for them when they ain't there.'

'There were three of them OK,' Kane insisted as he poured more amber liquor into his glass. 'They were star-packers and they made a real fight of it.'

Deacon stared at the whiskey in his glass. 'I just don't understand it, boys. It must have been the deputies known as Kid Palomino and Red Rivers. They must have returned early for some damn reason.'

A guilty hush fell over the four men. Then Deacon looked at the three figures and leaned against the back of his chair.

'I thought you were taking four men with you on this job, Bill,' he said as he glanced at Carson. 'What happened?'

Carson spat at the floor. 'Both the Brand boys got killed by them bastards, Deacon. I lost two good men.'

For the first time since his unexpected entrance, Danby Deacon looked troubled. He could not believe that his well-crafted plans had gone bad. He puffed on his cigar and then glanced at the three outlaws in turn.

'My plan would have meant that you could have entered and left Fargo without anyone noticing,' he said thoughtfully. 'By the time anyone figured that anything had happened you would have been long gone, but now things are different. Now there'll be a posse after you. They know what you've done and they'll come hunting to avenge that wrong, Bill.'

'I know, Deacon,' Carson sighed. 'What should we do?'

'Damned if I know.' Deacon shook his head, stood up and puffed frantically on his cigar as he looked down on the three men and the saddle-bags. 'I'm taking the next stagecoach out of here and putting distance between myself and them rope-twirlers. You boys can split my share of the money between yourselves. I don't want any part of it. I ain't getting lynched for what's in those saddle-bags.'

Bill Carson stood beside Deacon. 'There ain't another stagecoach coming through here until after sundown, Deacon. You're stuck here with me and the boys.'

Upon hearing the unwelcome news, Deacon suddenly looked sickly. 'We've got to get out of Dry Gulch before sunset, boys. We can't afford to waste the next couple of hours sitting around here waiting for those star-packers to arrive.'

'Our horses are spent, Deacon,' Carson growled as he grabbed the bottle and drank from its neck. As liquor dripped down his shirt front he lowered it and looked at the elegant Deacon. 'By the looks of it, you ain't even got a horse.'

'I didn't think I'd need one.' Deacon exhaled a line of smoke and pointed at Peters and Kane. 'Go try and round up four fresh horses for us. Pay anything they ask but get us four fresh mounts.'

Carson glared at them.

'You heard him. Get going and buy or steal us four fresh horses,' he raged. 'And be quick about it.'

Kane and Peters ran out into the brilliant sunshine leaving the two older men standing in the middle of the Busted Wheel.

'Do you reckon they'll find four fresh horses in

this shrivelled-up town, Bill?' Deacon asked the notorious Carson.

Carson shook his head. 'Nope, I sure don't, Deacon.'

FOURTEEN

Kid Palomino drew rein, stopped the high-shouldered stallion and rested his wrists on the horn of his saddle. The brilliant sunshine bathed Dry Gulch in a daunting glow, which alerted the young lawman that not everything was as it first appeared. The town seemed to be vacant of all life but Palomino knew that was not the case. Places near to the merciless desert harboured a different breed of people. They tended to shy away from venturing out into the rays of the cruel sun and waited for sundown before going about their business. Dry Gulch was similar to numerous others south of the border and the Kid was troubled by its apparent peacefulness. He stared thoughtfully at the small town from beneath the brim of his hat.

Red brought his quarter horse to a halt beside his younger companion and squinted at the array of wooden structures. The tin and wooden shingle rooftops could be seen sparkling in the distance as the overhead sun bore down upon them. The telegraph lines hung from their poles as they made their way to and from the bleached office in the centre of Dry Gulch.

'So that's Dry Gulch,' Red grunted as he steadied his thirsty mount. He was not impressed. 'The damn place looks deserted, Kid. I've seen ghost towns that look better than that.'

Palomino tilted his head and glanced at his sidekick.

'Nope, it ain't deserted, Red,' Palomino disagreed as he spotted two figures searching for something neither of the deputies could fathom. 'Do you see them galoots yonder?'

Red nodded. 'I see them.'

The younger deputy glanced at his partner.

'Now what do you figure them critters are doing running around in this heat, Red?' Palomino wondered as he stroked the lathered-up neck of his stallion.

'My bet is they're looking for something,' Red replied and checked the empty canteens hanging from his saddle horn. 'You got any water left, Kid?'

Palomino shook all of his canteens and then his head as he continued to focus on the fleeting glimpses of the outlaws as they crossed the town's main street. 'Sorry, pard. I'm clean out.'

Both their horses could smell the fresh water within the boundaries of the settlement. They strained at their leathers as both expert horsemen fought to restrain them.

'These nags know there's water real close, Kid,' Red said as he wrestled with his weary animal. 'They can smell it.'

Palomino nodded as his narrowed eyes kept watching the two distant men desperately continue their hunt. 'What in tarnation do you reckon them fellas are looking for?'

'Did you hear me?' Red repeated. 'These horses need water and we ain't gonna be able to stop them for much longer.'

'I hear you, Red,' the Kid sighed. 'What do you suggest?'

'We ain't got no choice, Kid.' Red straightened up on his saddle and pulled the brim of his hat down to shield his eyes from the dazzling sunlight. 'We gotta ride in there to water these nags.'

The Kid used every ounce of his remaining strength to hold the palomino stallion in check. 'I don't hanker riding straight in there and getting greeted by bullets, Red. I figure it might be smart on our part to circle the town and enter from behind them larger buildings yonder. We can use that gully to give us cover and get to water without being spotted by Carson and his cronies.'

Red sighed heavily. 'That's gonna tag another ten minutes on to us getting to water, Kid.'

'That's a whole lot better than getting picked off by Carson and his gang, ain't it?' Palomino turned the head of the tall mount beneath his saddle and tapped his spurs. The handsome cream-coloured horse began to walk slowly down into the long depression that encircled the town. 'C'mon. These animals got themselves a mighty big thirst.'

Reluctantly, the older lawman knew that his pal was right to be cautious. He gritted his teeth and shrugged as his gloved hands gripped the reins tightly.

'You're right, Kid.' Red allowed his horse to follow the younger horseman. They held their horses in check so that neither animal could bolt as the scent of the town's wells grew stronger.

As they journeyed along the sandy gully, they silently recalled the horrific sight that had brought them to this desolate place. Neither lawman had ever set eyes upon anything like the sickening outrage they had stumbled upon back in Fargo.

Images of the innocent people lying in pools of their own blood haunted them and continued to spur them on. The banker and the womenfolk had been slaughtered as though they were mere livestock being readied for the butcher's block.

The unholy memory of innocent, unarmed bodies lying in crimson pools of gore was branded into their minds and was impossible for them to shake off. Those memories would remain embedded in their minds forever.

Both Palomino and Red had silently resolved to get justice for those pitiful souls. It was the spur which drove them on toward their own possible destruction. Every sinew of their aching bodies screamed for them to stop but neither of the peace-keepers could quit now.

They had to prevent Carson and his equally depraved followers from continuing their merciless killing spree, even if it cost them their lives.

The tin stars pinned to their shirts gleamed like beacons in the bright sunlit gully as they secretly circled the small town of Dry Gulch. Palomino was dictating the pace they were travelling at, making sure that they did not cause dust to betray their presence.

'How far are we gonna go along this damn gully, Kid?' Red quietly asked his fellow deputy. 'I'm getting tuckered out holding this horse back, and no mistake.'

Palomino looked over his wide shoulder. 'Will you hush the hell up? I'm listening out for any sign of them murderous bastards, Red.'

They continued to slowly steer their mounts around the back of the few structures erected close to the heart of Dry Gulch. Then the younger deputy hauled back on his reins and stopped the tall stallion.

'What you stop for, Kid?' Red asked as he dragged back on his reins and halted the quarter horse.

'I'm gonna take me a look,' Palomino answered and then carefully balanced in his stirrups and stretched up to his full height so that he could see above the deep gully.

'What do you see, Palomino?' Red asked as he smoothed the neck of his tired horse and watched his friend.

Kid Palomino's eyes were half closed as they peeped over the sandy rim and observed the area. The back of the telegraph office was roughly twenty feet from the gully. Thirty feet to the side of the office, a far larger building dominated Dry Gulch. There was a full water trough set at the rear of the smaller office. The reflections of its precious contents danced across the wooden wall.

The young lawman lowered himself back down on his saddle and then he turned the palomino stallion to face his pal.

'We're right behind the telegraph office, Red,' the Kid said. 'It's got a trough out back.'

'What else did you see?' Red wondered.

'There's a tall building off to the left,' Palomino replied. 'I figure that must be a saloon.'

'Did you see their horses?'

The Kid shook his head, 'Nope, they must be out front.'

'Have we got cover, Kid?' Red asked.

'Yep, we've got plenty of cover, Red,' Palomino confirmed. 'Nobody will see us approach from here.'

'That's all I wanted to know.' Red tapped the flanks of his mount and rode around his friend. He studied the sandy slope and then jerked his reins hard and fast. The quarter horse cleared the side of the gully and reached the level ground behind the telegraph office. As the scarlet-whiskered horseman steadied his snorting horse, the Kid suddenly appeared right behind his quarter horse.

Palomino pointed at the rear of the smaller structure.

'We can tether the horses there,' he said as the

powerful stallion beneath him fought against its reins. 'Right next to the trough.'

Red nodded as they allowed their horses to walk toward the small weathered structure. The Kid dropped from his saddle first and looped his leathers around the metal pump beside the water trough.

Before Red had dismounted and secured his own mount, the Kid had drawn one of his trusty .45s and was investigating the area carefully.

His eyes darted from one building to another as they slowly headed into the very heart of the remote settlement.

'Seems awful quiet, Kid,' Red said as he stared through the shimmering heat at the array of buildings.

Palomino pressed his back against the side wall of the office and carefully looked around the corner of the sun-bleached building. His attention was drawn to the outlaws' three spent mounts tethered to the saloon's hitching rail.

'What you see, Kid?' Red asked as he leaned against his friend's shoulder.

'I see three lathered-up horses tied up outside the saloon, Red,' he answered before adding, 'I also see two critters in long dust coats. They're still looking for something.'

The bright sun was blazing down on the

loose-fitting coats worn by both Peters and Kane. Palomino suddenly felt his entire body go rigid as he spotted the bloodstains on the pale fabric.

The Kid knew that he was looking straight at the blood of the Hardwick clan. He lowered his head and shuddered as he felt his spine tingle.

'What's wrong, Kid?' Red asked his pal. 'You look like you just seen a ghost.'

The younger man looked down at his shorter friend.

'Maybe I have, you old rooster,' he sighed. 'Maybe I have.'

Red glanced around the corner of the telegraph office and watched as the outlaws went from one building to another. He scratched his head.

'What in tarnation are them *hombres* doing?' he wondered.

Palomino inhaled deeply. 'I reckon they're looking for something, Red. I just can't figure out what they're looking for.'

Red suddenly tapped his pal's arm. 'Their horses are spent, Kid. Look at them. They're plumb pitiful. Maybe them *hombres* are looking for fresh nags.'

Palomino considered his friend's words. 'You're probably right. Those horses sure look worse for wear. They wouldn't carry them outlaws far in that condition.'

Red rubbed his mouth on the back of his glove. 'If them two *hombres* are out in the sun hunting down fresh nags, Carson must be in the saloon on his lonesome, Kid.'

The notion of getting the drop on the infamous Bill Carson gave the Kid renewed vigour. A smile appeared from behind the mask of trail dust on his face. 'That's right, Red. He's on his lonesome in that drinking hole.'

'What we gonna do?' Red asked his pal.

The taller deputy swung around on his heels and led his pal back to where they had left their horses. He pointed the barrel of his gun at the side of the saloon. His eyes tightened as he studied the structure carefully.

'What you looking at, Kid?' the older deputy asked.

Palomino indicated to the veranda that encircled the wooden structure. Without answering, he grabbed his cutting rope from off his saddle and slid its coil over his arm.

'I got me an idea,' he drawled.

Red scratched his whiskers. 'What you need a rope for? You figuring on hanging them *hombres*?'

Palomino raised an eyebrow.

'Let's go pay that Carson varmint a visit,' he drawled.

Using the smaller telegraph office as cover the two men circled around the rear of the weathered structure and raced toward the Busted Wheel saloon.

FIFTEEN

Red Rivers soon found out what his partner needed his saddle rope for. No sooner had the lawmen reached the high-sided saloon than Palomino uncoiled his rope, swung it a few times and then launched it skyward. The lasso went clear of the wooden trimmings upon the veranda railings and then he pulled and tightened its loop. The slipknot loop constricted around one of the wooden adornments until it held firm. The Kid checked the rope with his weight and then glanced at Red.

'Ready?' Palomino grinned as he wrapped the slack around his arm and shoulder.

The older deputy shook his head and gulped.

'You ain't expecting me to climb up there, Kid?' Red exhaled at the daunting thought. 'Are you?'

Palomino shook his head. 'Nope, I reckon I'm about ten years too late to expect you to do that, Red.'

The older lawman shrugged. 'Then what?'

Suddenly all humour vanished from Palomino's face as he considered the daunting task ahead of them. He tightened the drawstring of his Stetson until it was tight under his chin. He pointed to the rear of the Busted Wheel.

'You make your way around the back of the saloon and find a way in, Red,' the Kid said as he gripped the rope and started to athletically ascend the wall. 'I need you to back up my play. Be careful how you enter this place, Red. Bill Carson can shoot the eye out of a meat-fly at a hundred paces, I'm told.'

'Don't go fretting, Kid.' Red gripped his six-shooter firmly and ran to the rear of the Busted Wheel. He had no idea what Kid Palomino intended to do but knew that whatever the Kid was intending, it was bound to be dangerous.

The Kid leaned back with the rope gripped firmly in his gloved hands and then started to ascend the wall. Within a few moments he had reached the railings and grabbed hold of one of them. Palomino threw his right leg over them and swiftly followed it on to the balcony. He loosened the rope and then began to coil it again as he stealthily made his way toward the front of the saloon.

Lowering his head so that his face was shielded from the bright sun he saw the two figures of Peters and Kane cross the street and head on to the back of the telegraph office.

'I hope they leave our horses alone,' Palomino whispered under his breath before continuing. He reached the weathered façade, which was nailed to the railings, then heard shouting from down the street. The Kid knew that it had to be the outlaws he had just witnessed heading to where he and Red had left their horses. He dropped on to one knee and squinted to where the raised voices were coming from.

Then he saw them.

Kane and Peters suddenly appeared from behind the telegraph office. As he watched them, the Kid knew why they were rejoicing. Just as he had figured, they had found both Red's quarter horse and his palomino stallion.

'Damn it all,' he cursed angrily as it dawned on him that if he were to unleash his guns on the brutal killers, the horses were in the line of fire. 'Why'd they have to find the horses?'

The Kid chewed on the thumb knuckle of his glove and watched the grinning men sat astride the horses as they slowly rode toward the saloon. Red had been correct. They were looking for replacement horses, just as his pal had guessed.

Palomino narrowed his eyes and glared down on Peters on his precious mount.

'You just made a real big mistake, fella,' he quietly fumed before carefully knotting the rope loop around the back of the railings. Then he frowned at Peters as he drew one of his matched Colts. 'Nobody rides Nugget without my permission.'

Dust drifted up from the hoofs of the walking horses as they steadily closed the distance between themselves and the Busted Wheel.

Suddenly the jubilation both outlaws felt in discovering the two handsome animals evaporated. Jeff Kane hauled back on the reins of the quarter horse as he caught a brief glimpse of the lawman behind the decaying saloon name board. He glanced across to tell his fellow outlaw of what he had just spied but Peters had already spotted the Kid. Kane steadied the muscular animal beneath him as Peters slowly slipped one of his six-shooters from its holster.

'You seen him too, Poke?' Kane asked.

Poke Peters gave a slow nod of his head as he screwed his eyes up tight and watched the vague shadow behind the long name board.

'Yep, I seen the sun dancing off his tin star a few yards back.' Poke Peters pulled back on the hammer of his .45 and then suddenly raised it. 'Whoever that is, he's a dead man.'

The entire town rocked as the bullet flashed through the shimmering heat and punched a fist-sized hole in the façade beside the crouching Palomino.

A thousand red-hot splinters blasted into Palomino's face without warning. It was like being consumed by angry fire-ants. The deputy yelled out in pain and rolled across the floorboards to the end of the Busted Wheel name board. Half blinded by the sudden shock, the Kid lifted his six-shooter and blasted a wild shot down at the horsemen.

Undeterred by the deafening reply of Palomino's wild gunshot, Peters and Kane fanned their gun hammers again, sending chunks of debris rising up into the air from the wooden railings.

The Kid rubbed the side of his face with his gloved fingers until he was able to open his eyes. It was like staring through a waterfall as the singed lawman crawled even further away from where bullets continued to rip the saloon sign apart.

'Do you figure we got him, Poke?' Kane shouted above the deafening din.

Peters shook his head as his eyes searched the length of the balcony. 'Keep shooting until we see the blood dripping, Jeff.'

Like hounds with a cornered racoon, the outlaws refused to quit. They kept firing their guns up at the balcony whilst the Kid dodged the deadly lead like a matador sidestepping a raging bull.

Palomino spat on to the tails of his bandanna and pressed them against his eye in a vain bid to soothe the fire that raged inside it. He blinked hard and could just see the devilish pair as they fired up at him.

He ducked and crawled beneath the red-hot tapers.

The choking smoke from the outlaws' guns hung in the arid air as Palomino curled his finger around the trigger of his .45. Yet no matter how hard he strained to see clearly, an agonizing pain burned like a branding iron into his eye.

He cursed.

All he could make out for certain was the blurred images of the riders below his vantage point. He moved his barrel away from the golden stallion and toward his partner's smaller mount.

'If I get this wrong, Red can always buy a new quarter horse but if I accidentally shoot my palomino . . .' the Kid reasoned as bullets continued to keep him pinned down. 'Aim high and you shouldn't hit Red's horse.'

Defying the agony which racked his face, the Kid

cocked, aimed and fired his gun at Kane. To his surprise he saw the outlaw buckle as scarlet gore exploded from his back. Palomino ducked as Peters' avenging bullets narrowly missed him. When there was a lull in the barrage of gunshots the Kid fired his Colt at the wounded Kane again. The outlaw jerked violently on the saddle as the second shot finished him off for good. A sickening groan escaped from Kane's deathly lips as he tumbled from the saddle and fell limply into the ground beside the quarter horse's hoofs.

'Jeff!' Peters screamed out in horror as he stared down at the gruesome sight. Yet no matter how loud he yelled, there was no reply. The outlaw dragged the neck of the palomino around and stared up at the long balcony.

He shook the spent casings from his gun before reloading the smoking chambers.

'You're gonna pay for that, star-packer,' Peters raged and then glared through the dazzling sunlight to where he had first spotted Palomino. He hastily started firing again at the saloon sign above him.

Palomino threw himself across the balcony as bullets shattered the glass of the second storey windows. The injured star-packer kept rolling until he had returned to his cutting rope behind the bullet-ridden façade.

He gripped the rope and lowered his head as more choking splinters cascaded over his hunched shoulders. Clouds of black smoke gave the deputy cover as he rose up to his full height and moved with the rope in one hand and his gun in the other.

He cocked his gun hammer and trained it at Peters. The trouble was his weeping eyes still could not clearly see his target. The Kid was just about to fire his smoking six-shooter when it dawned on him that he might end up missing the outlaw and shoot his precious palomino stallion instead.

Another shot came within inches of him. The Kid could feel the heat of the bullet and staggered sideways. He shouted at the top of his lungs at his obedient mount.

'Punch them stars, Nugget boy,' he yelled down at his horse. 'Rise and punch them stars.'

The magnificent stallion did exactly as its master commanded and reared up and kicked its forelegs out just as it had been trained to do. Peters was caught by surprise and found himself toppling backwards. The outlaw dropped his gun and grabbed at the saddle horn. As the palomino stallion landed its hoofs back on to the sand, Peters went to drag his other six-gun from his belt.

It was too late.

Kid Palomino had already launched himself off the balcony holding on to his rope. He swung wide and low through the smoke-filled air.

Both the Kid's boots hit the outlaw squarely in the back sending him flying over the golden mane of the palomino stallion. Peters crashed heavily into the ground with the fearless lawman just behind him. Palomino released his grip on the rope and leapt on to the winded Peters. He grabbed the outlaw's hair and dragged it toward him.

The dazed Peters tried to reach up and grab the deputy but Palomino clenched a fist and smashed his knuckles into Peters' jaw. The sound of knuckle on jawbone echoed along the street.

For a moment the Kid thought that he had knocked the outlaw out but Peters was not so easily subdued. He twisted on his side, wrapped his legs around his opponent's and caused the Kid to fall.

Palomino could not see his foe clearly but he could feel his punches as they pounded into him. The tables had somehow been reversed. Peters leapt on to the Kid and sent a right cross into the deputy's head. He then grabbed Palomino's shoulders and wrestled him full circle.

Both battling men feverishly grappled with one another as they slowly rose to their feet. The Kid grabbed Peters as the outlaw sent punch after punch into his midriff.

Then suddenly the quiet street resounded to the deafening sound of gunfire. The Kid stared over Peters' shoulder and saw the unmistakable figure of Bill Carson standing in front of the saloon's swing doors. Even his blurred vision could not mistake the infamous outlaw as he emptied his gun in his direction.

Without realizing it, the young lawman had somehow positioned Poke Peters between himself and Carson's deadly bullets. He felt the impact of every shot as they drilled into Peters' back. The young outlaw rocked under the impact of the merciless lead. Finally Poke Peters fell into Palomino's arms as his pitiful face looked at the Kid in utter disbelief.

Peters went to speak but the only thing that left his lips was blood. His eyes rolled back and vanished under his lids. He sighed heavily as life departed him and slumped into the arms of the Kid.

Bill Carson stepped down into the sunlight as he reloaded his trusty gun and looked admiringly at the palomino stallion standing in the street beside the quarter horse. He then glanced over his shoulder and shouted at Deacon.

'Looks like we got ourselves some horseflesh after all, Deacon,' he chuckled in his usual sickly manner.

'A quarter horse for you and a high-shouldered beauty for me. Come take a looksee.'

Danby Deacon reluctantly pushed the swing doors apart and left the confines of the Busted Wheel. He moved after the confident outlaw. 'Has the shooting stopped, Bill?'

Carson snapped the chamber of his smoking gun and spun its cylinder as he glared at Kid Palomino standing behind the bullet-ridden Peters.

'The shooting's nearly stopped, Deacon,' he drawled as he cocked the gun and aimed it at the head of the youthful star-packer. 'There's just one more varmint I've gotta put out of its misery. Then we can ride out of this town with the loot.'

Palomino was holding the lifeless Poke Peters upright with both hands. It took every scrap of his strength. He knew that it was impossible to release his grip and draw one of his guns before Carson fired.

'Tell me one thing,' Carson growled as he closed the distance between them. 'Who in tarnation are you? You've bin a real pain in my arse.'

'He's Kid Palomino, Carson,' Red shouted out from behind both Deacon and Carson as he pushed his way through the swing doors and stood with his cocked gun in his hand. 'Now drop that hog-leg before I drop you.'

Bill Carson lowered his head thoughtfully and then sighed as he stared at the smoking gun in his hand.

FINALE

Deacon turned and ran toward Red with his hands clasped together as though in prayer. He fell on to his knees and pleaded to the lawman, 'Help me. I don't know who this man is, Deputy. He and his cronies ambushed me. They're monsters and I'm just a simple gambler. Please save me.'

As Red considered the outpouring, Bill Carson turned on his heels with his six-shooter at hip height and glared at Deacon in disgust. He glared at the man who until now had never given him any reason to doubt his word.

'You stinking liar,' Carson hissed like a sidewinder and then fired straight into the back of the kneeling Deacon. As the criminal mastermind arched and fell lifelessly on to his face, Red squeezed his own trigger and sent a bullet into the centre of Carson's chest.

The outraged outlaw staggered across the sand coughing up bloody spittle with every step. His vicious eyes glared at Red as he steadied himself. 'You shouldn't have done that, star-packer.'

Red dragged his hammer back with his thumb as he watched Carson muster every ounce of his dwindling energy to raise his gun-hand again.

'Drop that gun, Carson,' Red shouted at the outlaw.

The veteran outlaw did not listen. He cocked the hammer of his gun again and stared with deathly eyes at the man with the tin star gleaming on his chest. 'That was a real big mistake, star-packer. I'm dead but so are you.'

Fearing for the safety of his friend, Palomino swiftly released his hold on the lifeless Peters and drew his own .45 in one fluid action. He repeatedly fanned the gun hammer and sent the last of its bullets into Bill Carson.

The outlaw swayed as his gun fell from his hand and landed in the sand heavily. His eyes snaked between the two men wearing the tin stars. Carson spat blood at the ground as life slowly left his bullet-ridden torso. He flinched in agony while death gripped his torrid soul in its unforgiving fingers. He then stumbled and he fell.

It was like watching a tree falling.

Dust rose around the body and hung in the dry air as Palomino limped across to his pal, patted him on the arm and then sat down on the weathered boardwalk. He removed his gloves and started to reload his gun with bullets from his belt.

'Where's the bank money, Red?' the Kid asked wearily.

'On a card table inside the saloon, Kid,' Red sighed and slid his gun back into its holster. 'I passed it on the way here.'

'How come you took so long?' Palomino asked wryly. 'I nearly got myself killed out here before you showed.'

Red rubbed his scarlet whiskers. 'You told me to be careful, Kid. I was being careful.'

Palomino chuckled and pushed the chamber back into the body of his Colt. 'That's true, I did tell you to be careful.'

Red walked to both their horses and led them to the trough next to the outlaws' spent mounts. He wrapped their long leathers around the hitching pole and secured them before resting a boot on the step of the boardwalk.

'By my figuring we got them all, Palomino,' he said as he pulled his tobacco pouch from his shirt pocket and started to sprinkle the contents on to the gummed paper.

Kid Palomino got to his feet as the sound of pounding hoofs echoed around the weathered structures. He leaned over the trough and splashed water into his face to soothe his sore eye. He straightened up and stared at the five horsemen as they entered Dry Gulch.

'Sheriff Lomax is finally here with his posse, Red,' he sighed before stepping up on to the boardwalk and placing a hand on the swing doors. 'C'mon. I'll buy you a beer.'

Red rubbed his chin and poked the twisted cigarette in the corner of his mouth. 'Do you reckon that fancy-looking dude lying in the dust is the *hombre* Carson got all his information from, Kid?'

Palomino scratched a match across his belt buckle and lit his partner's cigarette. As smoke drifted from Red's mouth the Kid tossed the match at the sandy street.

'Yep, I sure do.' He nodded and walked into the saloon with his pal a step behind him.

'Come to think about it I seen him about two weeks back playing poker in Fargo, Kid.' Red pulled the cigarette from his lips and blew smoke at the sawdust-covered floor. 'He sure was a mighty bad poker player.'

'It don't matter none, Red,' Palomino smiled. 'Not where he's headed.'

The posse pulled up outside the Busted Wheel as the two deputies reached the bar and rested their aching bones against its wooden counter. They glanced at the swollen satchels of the three saddle-bags on the card table and then Palomino nodded to the tall man polishing glasses behind the bar.

'A couple of tall beers, barkeep,' Palomino told the bartender before noticing the pained expression on his pal's face. 'What's troubling you, Red?'

Red glanced at his friend.

'How come Sheriff Lomax always arrives after the shooting's ended, Kid?' Red sighed as he sucked smoke into his lungs.

Kid Palomino thought for a moment then shook his head and shrugged. 'I reckon that's one mystery we'll never be able to figure, Red.'

Hyram Smith placed the two tall beers down and watched as the deputies lifted the glasses and tapped them together.

'For Charlie,' Palomino toasted.

'Charlie,' Red nodded.